Rembrandt

BLOOD BROTHERHOOD BOOK 1

KATHI S. BARTON

WCP

World Castle Publishing, LLC
Pensacola, Florida

Copyright © Kathi S. Barton 2015
Print ISBN: 9781629891965
eBook ISBN: 9781629891972
First Edition World Castle Publishing, LLC, January 9, 2015
http://www.worldcastlepublishing.com

Licensing Notes

Cover Art: Karen Fuller
Photographer: Xie4to-graphy
Cover Model: Ethan Dean
Editor: Eric Johnston

Chapter 1

Remy dropped to his knees, slamming his bloodied sword into the stained earth at his feet. His armor—chest plate and leggings—were covered in the blood of his enemies. Under it, against his battered body, his blood soaked his skin. Blood and sweat dripped down his back and over open wounds that would never heal in his lifetime. He knew as surely as he knelt there that he was as good as dead.

"Do not be so hasty, my friend." Remy looked up. His left eye was either swollen shut or missing, so it was difficult for him to focus well. "Rembrandt, you have been a good man. Now is not the time for you to give up."

"I have nothing left to give. I am finished." The man laughed, and Remy felt something akin to fear race over his skin. "I wish only to lie here and let my blood spill upon the ground. My life...I have nothing left in me that I wish to go on for."

"I have heard about your wife and children. It is sad when there is so much death during a war. But for the young and innocent to die like they had...well, it is not what war should be." Remy felt the pain of their death again. Fresh as the day he'd found their broken and burned bodies. "I have a need for your services. You will help me, yes?"

"Nay." He tried to stand, but it was too much for him, so he leaned heavily against his sword. He was hurt beyond what was reasonable for a man. He'd been nearly dead twice this day, and he was going to let the wound in him do its worst. "I've a pike in my back that is through me. More broken bones than a person should have and still be upright. My blood spills upon the earth even as we speak. I've done my share. The war within me is over. I should like to die."

"Do you not see the carnage that goes on now? Look around you, young Rembrandt. Even now, the dying are being converted into beings that will someday kill all that matters to everyone. They will walk the earth for many more years than need be. They will be more of an enemy than you have fought this day." Remy closed his eyes against the words. He had no idea what the man spoke of and really, if he was honest with himself, no longer cared. "But you do, my good man. You always have."

"What magic is this you use? I have not spoken aloud to you. I have not said these words that you answer as if you know them." The man reached.

The magic touched his sight first. He looked around the battlefield and saw the bodies, some he knew, others he did not, lay back-to-back, head-to-toe all around him. The only spot where there was nothing was where he now knelt, and soon it would be filled with him.

"See them beyond." He looked harder, squinting to see the men…no, not men, but things going from body to body. Lifting up some that had movement, ignoring the dead for the living. Remy watched in horror as they looked as if they were eating them. Tearing into their throats as if they were a meal to have. "They do not eat them, Remy, but feed upon their blood. And when they finish, have taken all that they have had to offer them, they will convert them into what they are. Monsters that will rule the world if not for men like you. It is what I have come to you about."

Remy looked at him then. He was dressed all in black and carried a black cane with a silver tip. His dark hair hung over his shoulder in a braid that seemed to be streaked with red. Remy looked away from him. For some reason it hurt him to look.

"I have told you now thrice I have nothing to give you. I am sorry for these men or whatever they are, but I have no will to go on." Remy watched as one of his own men was taken to the mouth of one of the creatures. He had fought a good fight but lost when the creature snapped him in half and drank from him anyway. When he was dropped to the ground, Augustus sat up and looked right at him. Then he stretched and began searching the bodies as well.

"Augustus Hill will kill many more than any of the other men that are changed this day. There will be times when he will sneak into the rooms of the innocent and tear out their throats simply because he can. They will die because he will be more than we've accounted for. Much more. He is not a true creature."

"I don't understand." The man just smiled at him, and Remy looked away again. He'd seen something there, within his mouth, that frightened him. "You speak of things that you cannot expect me to understand or do a thing about. I am dying."

"No longer." He looked at him again. This time he was sure he saw the long, sharp teeth there. "You see what I wish for you to see. The fangs are to help me feed upon humans, as you will. And I have...let us just say that I have already completed your transformation. You will rise up now and begin the task that I have come for you to do."

"Nah. I will not do as you request." The man stood up and pulled Remy with him. The pike that had been run through him hours ago was pulled from his body, and he didn't feel anything but the sliding of it leaving his body. All his pains were gone, he noticed, his body seemingly whole. "What have you done to me?" He reached for the man as he had millions of times over the years and came up with only air.

Remy woke with a start. The dream again. He was forever having the man who had changed his life invade his dreams. It had been more years, more decades and beyond than he liked to think about. And as soon as he saw him again, he was planning to kill him.

The bed he was in shifted slightly, and he pulled the naked flesh to his cock. The ass was warm, and he rocked his cock into the crevice that was there. The woman behind him reached between him and the woman at his front and fisted him. His cock stretched to feel the warmth around it.

"You are a healthy man, aren't you?" She had no idea, he thought to himself. "I should like to ride you again if you are willing. A thick cock like this can go a long way to filling a woman."

Before he could answer her, Remy found himself on his back. She was sliding over him as the woman to his left rolled over. Her breasts were round and full, the woman sliding her pussy over him just as full but not as heavy. He cupped her and pulled hard on her nipple. Her moan had Remy rocking harder into the pussy riding him.

"Come to my mouth. I wish to feast as I am being taken." The woman hurried to do as he bid her. Her pussy was wet, and her clit swollen already as she moved over his mouth. Remy would feed from her here. She'd never know that he took not only her cum but her blood as well. It was the best meal he'd take.

He held her to him as he ate at her. When she came, and it was almost too quick for him to enjoy her, his mouth was flooded with not just her sweet juices but her blood as well when he sank his fangs into her warmed flesh. Her second climax had her grinding hard against his mouth and tongue, and Remy drank greedily. He sealed her wounds and moved her aside as the woman at his cock cried out. He moved so he could sink his teeth into her throat as his cocked empty into her mouth.

Remy held them both when they fell into a deep sleep. His cock still throbbed with need, and he cupped himself tightly in his fist. Before he could bring himself to any kind of relief, one of the women put her hand over his and finished him off with her mouth. Remy laid there basking in the post-sexual bliss after she rolled away from him.

"Will you be in town long?" The first woman, who had gotten up an hour later, stood near the bed with nothing but her panties on as she spoke softly to him. "I could stay all day if you want. I've never had a man between my legs that could give so much pleasure before taking his own."

"Nay, I leave today." He pulled her to him again and suckled at her breast. She curled her fingers into his hair and held him to her as he nipped at her deeply and drank again. When he lifted his head, there was no trace of what he'd done on either her flesh or in her mind. "You will be safe by not roaming the streets again. Find yourself another line of work and not on your back."

Her nod had her pulling away from him. He had probably just cost her pimp a great deal of money by telling her not to do this again. When he did the same for the second woman, she too nodded and he felt good about it for a few minutes. As surely as he'd taken them from the streets, he knew that it was only a matter of time before something else took their lives. The malefactors were becoming stronger every day. Stronger than he could fight off.

After they left him, Remy went into the bathroom. He turned on the shower to its hottest setting and looked in the mirror. He looked the same as he did on the day he'd buried his wife and three children.

Remy had always been a warrior. He'd fought in wars that he no longer knew the cause he'd been fighting for. There were days, many of them as a matter of fact, that he wished that the man in black had never found him. It was his wish now, after all these years that he'd taken his own life on the day he'd found his family as he'd thought of doing.

"But it is too late now." He stepped into the water and felt the burn of it on his skin. The body that he had now, the one he'd left the final field with was stronger than he'd been. His muscles were thick along his arms and chest. His legs were thickly corded with them, and he knew that any wound that he'd take would be gone within seconds of them being put upon him.

As he finished his bath, he thought about his day. Today he was to find a man by the name of Davis Brown.

He needed to add another person to his group of fighters, and he'd heard great things about the man. Remy was pulling on his pants when he felt someone in the room with him. He turned slowly, knowing that anyone who dared to intrude on his peace was as good as dead.

"Hello, Rembrandt." The man in black sat on the sofa and looked around the room. "You have done well then? Making the world a better place?"

"I hoped you dead." The man only threw back his head in mirth. "When you left me, you said my services would end. But you never said when."

"I have still a need of a man with your powers. And you have a good deal of them, don't you, Rembrandt? Many more than anyone, including your men know about." Remy said nothing. He was still finding things that he could do daily. It was as if he gained more with each malefactor he killed. "You do, you know. Gaining will keep you ahead of them. But I have come to reward you."

"My death then." The man shook his head and smiled at him. "There is no other reward I wish for. You know that I have longed to join my wife and children. There is nothing here for me."

"Ah, but there is." Remy sat down and pulled on his boots. It was, as far as he was concerned, the greatest invention he'd known man to come up with. Leather boots that kept your feet dry and your legs safe. "Rembrandt, are you not even curious as to what reward you will gain?"

"Nay, I am not." When he tied his last boot, he stood up. "Nor do I have any wish to be with you this morn. I have a meeting."

"Mr. Brown will serve you well. As the other men in your troupe. I have a list of them, others that I should like for you to bring into your fold." Remy didn't bother saying anything. But it was on his mind to tell him that he had no wish to hire Davis to work for him, simply because he had said so. "You are still as stubborn as you were so many years ago."

"Eighteen hundred and forty-four to be precise. A man should not live to be so old. I am tired." He wasn't but that didn't matter. He was exhausted with living. That was all. "What is this reward that you think I would want from you? Be quick about it so that I may get on with my work you put upon me."

"The locket around your neck? Does it still hold the image of your wife and children?" Remy growled. "I mean no disrespect, Rembrandt. I only ask if the image of them still holds your heart. You lie with other women, so I know that your need is still there. But the love of them, will you ever think to replace it?"

"Never." The man nodded and stood up. "You will leave me to my peace? You will give me my reward of death?"

"No. But I do leave you with the names of others. Men that will join you, not just work for you." He didn't understand the difference and said so. "These will be men that will be at your back, help you when you need it and will become good friends that you will need in the coming months."

The slip of paper fell to the floor as the man disappeared. Remy didn't bother picking it up. He had no use for men that the man in black recommended. The few that helped him, mostly humans he could find with some strength, died almost before they were trained. Remy left the hotel room the same way he'd entered, by way of his magic.

Davis was sitting where he'd asked him to meet him. There were malefactors everywhere, and they wove in and out of the humans as the air did around them. When he sat at the table, two brave ones, malefactors who were too new to know who he was, came just close enough to them that Remy was able to kill one with the tip of his sword and behead him even before the other knew what he was about. The second one Remy grabbed around the neck and held.

"You have been warned, have you not?" The creature snarled at him and showed him the mouth of sharp fangs that made his so different than him. Remy opened his mouth wide and let him see that he too could bite and snapped his together in the monster's face.

"You have yourself a right nasty thing there." He looked at Davis and wondered about the man. "I just snap their necks, but that doesn't seem to keep them down. How do you do it?"

"You have to tear their hearts out while it still beats within their chest." It was true that they could be killed this way, but not the only one. And Davis seemed to know it. But the monster in his hand didn't. He could feel his fear as if he owned it. "Sometimes I like to play with them before I dispatch them away. But not today. We need to speak. Is that all right?"

Davis leaned back in his chair and nodded. Remy looked at the monster, then smiled when it started to hiss and growl. There was no way it could escape his grip, and he only squeezed tighter.

He'd been dealing with these things for so long that they no longer made him think of them as anything but an annoying bug. Reaching his hand into the throat of the thing, he felt his neck break and his body struggle for breath. Not that the thing needed it any more than Remy did, but habits were hard to break. As soon as he touched his lungs, Remy grabbed onto one of them closest to the heart and pulled. The thing lay at his feet as Remy dropped the mess on him. Remy looked around.

No one could see him or Davis. And only a very select few could see the malefactors. He supposed it was a good thing. If humans could see what stalked them, they might never leave their homes. Not that it did them any good. They could enter a house as easily as he could if he wanted to gain entrance.

The screams of the other malefactors nearly had him wince. Remy knew that if you showed them any sort of acknowledgement, they would use it relentlessly. Instead, he watched them as they gathered their dead and flew out of the restaurant. The humans around the room had no idea how he'd saved some of them.

"I'm going to work with you." Remy shook his head but said nothing as Davis continued. "This man came to see me. Dressed all in black. He said that no matter your terms, I was to work with you. I'm willing to do that after what I just saw."

"It's hard work. Dangerous too. And you might be better off simply staying where you are." Davis shook his head this time and smiled. "He touch you? Give you something that would make you more than you are now?"

"He did. I lay dying in my bed when he came to see me a few weeks back. Cancer was eating its way through me as if it were having a fine meal. But the man told me that I was needed. Nobody ever needed me in my whole life. But I told him that I would do what I could with the time I had left. He said that I had plenty of time and that I was to hunt you down. Said you go by Rembrandt and nothing more." Remy nodded and told him to call him Remy. "All right then, Remy. What do we do now?"

Remy had no idea and said as much. "I roam the streets and kill what I find. Save the humans from their ignorance and move to the next group of them. It is a hard task, lonely at times. The pay is good, but you've no time to spend it."

Davis laughed. "Much like my old job. I was a cop. One of the good ones. I never thought…when that man left me I felt like I'd been given a great gift. Strength like I've never had. The ability to do things that I've never been able to do before. Feeding, as he called it, is not so bad. The sex that comes with it is better than I thought a man like me would ever get."

Remy started to speak when a woman came to their table. He had kept them away from them. No humans could see them at all unless he wanted them to. Yet here she stood. When he looked up at her, Remy could see her confusion, but her voice was strong and clear.

"He said you forgot this in your haste to leave today." He asked her who. "I'm sorry, I don't know. But he gave me a thousand dollars to make sure you took it this time. Please take it, mister. I could really use the extra money."

He didn't want to take it. To take it meant that he'd have to do it. He'd have to find the other men on this list and work with them. But the woman looked at him so earnestly that he snatched it from her. When she smiled at him, Remy had a feeling that he'd been had. As soon as she turned, she disappeared in a puff of smoke.

There were five names on the paper besides Davis's. The writing was a beautiful script that made him think of his lovely mother and her bending over him to teach him to read and write. The first name on the list was marked through. Even he could tell that it had been Davis Brown. Remy handed the paper to Davis.

"Nathaniel Livingston, Richard Harmon, Christopher Alexander, and Leonard Earl." He handed it back to him. "I don't know these men. Do you?"

"No. But I have a feeling we'll know them soon enough." Remy was pissed off. Not a state of mind he liked to be in. When he was mad, he tended to do stupid things. And right now he could see a colossal fuck up coming his way. He stood when Davis did.

"I will have to find us lodgings. I would assume that there is a house around that would work?" Davis asked him if they'd be living together. "I think it would suit us best if we did. Training would be foremost. Then there is the added advantage that we could keep an eye out for each other. I think it would be best."

"There's this big warehouse over on Madison Avenue. It will need some work, more than likely a shit load of work. I could look into that for us." Remy nodded and they made their way out of the restaurant. "We'll need some supplies as well. Things that we're not going to be able to get at the local Wally-World."

"Guns." Davis nodded. "I'll take care of those. As well as any other weapons you can think of. Oh and a staff. I think we should make us look like we're a household and not a bunch of vampires in a nest."

"We're vampires?" Remy shrugged. They were what most thought of as vamps. They fed from humans to survive. They healed quickly and lived forever. The only thing that was different that he could see is that they didn't need to avoid the sun. In fact, he'd been known to sun on the beach when he'd been looking for malefactors.

As soon as they exited the building, the man in black appeared. He would have walked past him had he been able, but the man reached out and touched his arm. The burn of it, the incredible pain brought him to his knees. Remy was leaning over to puke, a thing he'd not done in centuries when he noticed that Davis was there as well, his body inert on the ground and blood pouring from his nose. Remy tried to see if he too was bleeding when he was suddenly free, his body upright before he could stand on his own.

"You belong to me now." The man laughed. The sound of it echoing around in his head as he disappeared. Remy helped Davis to stand and saw the markings on his arm. Rolling up his sleeve, Remy noticed that he too was marked, but with a different symbols.

Both of them, leaning heavily on each other, made their way to the alley beside the restaurant. Davis pulled his shirt off and looked down at his chest. Remy only stared. There were ancient markings all over his chest and arms. Remy had a feeling that he was going to look just as inked.

"Do you know what this is?" Remy shook his head. "I'm guessing that we're in some sort of club together now. He said that I belonged to him."

"He said the same to me." Remy leaned back against the wall behind him. "I do not wish to belong to him. I wish I had never met him."

"I'm thinking it's a little too late for that." Remy thought so as well. "I feel good. Better than I did before and that was fucking fantastic. You?"

"Yes. Stronger. I have…there are things buzzing in my head that was not there before. Knowledge of things that I suppose will help me, help us." Davis nodded. "The other men, the ones on the list, do you suppose that they will be marked as we are?"

"If not now, then when we find them for sure." Remy thought so as well. "We'll need to get things in order. I believe…I don't know why, but I think we are about to go to war."

Davis said he'd get on the building, and they exchanged phone numbers. As soon as they parted ways, Remy looked back. He could feel the man's thoughts. He wondered if he could also feel his and thought not. Something had happened to them both, and he was afraid it was going to be more of a hindrance than a help.

"So untrusting, Rembrandt. Why are you like this?" Remy ignored the voice in his head and moved toward where he knew he could get guns and weapons. *"You will call to me when you are ready. I still have your reward to give you."*

Remy didn't want a reward. He didn't want anything to do with any of this. When he made contact with his seller, he bought all he had and then some. He even placed an order for a large shipment of silver and turquoise.

Chapter 2

Skylar took the man his coffee and walked back to the counter. The man gave her the creeps, but he tipped well. Not like most jerks that only came in for a cup of brew. When Tommy, the bus boy, asked her if she was ready to go home, she shook her head and nodded to the man in black.

"You go on home. I'll lock up." He looked over at the man, then back at her. "He's harmless. I've been here before with him at closing."

"I got a test tomorrow. If you don't mind too much, I'm gonna take you up on it." She told him to get going and good luck. "Thanks. Just four more weeks of school and I'm out. Then I'm going to spend the rest of my life paying for a college education that will do me no good."

"You're going to be a great accountant." He snorted at her. "You saved me a ton of money last year doing my taxes. I'm hoping you do the same this time."

"You don't make any money and you pay out a lot. It was simple." She knew that. Up until the day he'd done it, she'd been doing her own. But he'd asked her if she wanted him to do them and she'd not been able to turn him down. "I'll see you tomorrow."

After Tommy left she locked the door. This was the third time this week that the man in black had been here after closing. She wondered if he was stalking her but decided that he could do a lot better than her. Skylar Manning was not the type of woman that men like him went after. She was more of the good-friend-next-door type.

"If you would be so kind, may I have a refill?" Skylar picked up the fresh pot of coffee and took it to his table. The man was so...strange, she thought, but very handsome too. As she refilled his cup, she had a sudden thought that he was dangerous. So when he put out his hand to her, she backed away.

"I'm sorry. I just...I just realized how stupid I am to be here with you." His smile did strange things to her, bad things. Terrible things. Fear now raced along her skin, and she had a feeling that he was going to hurt her. "Don't. Please? I have nothing that you'd want."

"Oh, but you do, my dear. You most certainly do. But I will not harm you. Not at all. But I should like to give you something." She shook her head and backed away. "It will not hurt you but will keep you safe."

"No thanks." When she was far enough away from him that she could go to the coffee maker without coming close to him, she sat the hot pot on the burner and turned it off. "I think you need to leave now. It's past closing time."

He stood up but didn't move to the door. "Skylar, if you do not take what I have to offer you, when you leave here you will die. And I have a profound need for you to meet someone."

"It's time you left." As she made her way to the door to let him out, she grabbed the Louisville slugger under the counter as she went. "If you touch me, I'm going to bash your skull in and piss on your dead body."

"Such spirit. Strength that will aid you, I think. And my young man will fall head over heels in love with you." He nodded and moved to the door, his dark and silver cane tapping on the floor as he went. "My good friend…well, he is not a friend, but a man who I employ. He will be most displeased that you come to harm. It is his fault I believe that this should come to pass. Had he started at the top of the list, as I had indicated, then you would be safe from harm. But he too is a stubborn person, and both of you shall have to live with it."

When he was at the door, she backed up. It occurred to her that he could still reach her with his cane, so she put out her bat to keep him away. He only smiled at her as he walked through the doorway. But he turned at the last second and grabbed her arm.

"It will only hurt but a moment." She screamed then. The pain running up her arm seemed to burn all over her. Her head felt as if he'd hit her with the cane, yet it still rested on the floor at his feet. She knew this because it was all she could focus on while the pain riddled her body. When he let her go, she fell forward and threw up twice before she lay down and curled into a ball. Everything, every part of her seemed to have been branded by the man. Closing her eyes, she let the pain roll through her until she was lost in blackness.

When she could finally stand up after waking, she looked around. The door was closed and locked, and her mess, her dinner had been cleaned up as well. Even her bat was back where she'd pulled it from as if she'd never touched it. Skylar tried to tell herself that it had all been a dream, that she'd only hit her head, but she knew that the man had hurt her in ways that no man had before. Skylar was shaking so badly that she had to lean on the tables to make her way back to her things. Once there she set the alarm, then walked back to the front. Her body was feeling much better, but her arm, her right one, was still burning. Leaving the deposit for tomorrow, she left the diner in favor of her home.

"See if I wait on your ass again." Skylar turned the keys in the lock and started for home. She didn't live in the best of neighborhoods, but she'd never felt threatened before. Tonight for some reason she did. Every shadow made her heart beat a little harder.

Skylar was only a block from her apartment when she realized she was being followed. Pausing at the crosswalk just a little longer, she turned back to see a person move into the shadows of the building he was near. Her heart felt now like it was at her throat, and she tried to think what to do. Calling the police would do her no good. They didn't come to this neighborhood unless it was necessary, and she'd yet to figure out what that might be. Instead she moved a little quicker to her home. The man looked…well, he looked like a black and white photo.

At the bottom of the steps, someone grabbed her from behind. She wasn't sure who was more surprised when he turned her around to face him, but she was pretty sure she was more afraid. Skylar wasn't sure what he was but he couldn't be real. When he opened his mouth, she knew a real kind of fear.

"You are chosen for greatness." His breath hissed over her skin like a hot fire. "It will taste so good to have you. I will be much envied when they know I have had you."

"Oh yeah. Well, fuck off, buddy. I am not going to let you touch me." He looked down at where his hand was on her arm, and she felt it heat up. When he jerked back from her, his hand smoking, she moved back a few steps to run. But he grabbed her again. This time she knew he was in pain.

"You will cease this and allow me my due." She had no clue what he meant and reached into her pocket for her mace. Before she could pull it out and use it, someone touched her from behind.

"You will only piss him off if you do that." The thing in front of her hissed at the man behind her, and she heard him laugh. "You are in the wrong place at the wrong time, malefactor. Where is the rest of your clique?"

"I have no timepiece." A burble of laughter spilled from Skylar's mouth before she could think about it getting her killed. The thing in front of her slapped her, sending her back into the man behind her and then to the ground. Her face felt as if she'd been hit by a wall, a big one at that. Then the pain was gone. Standing up, she looked behind her at the man who had been behind her.

"Christ." He bowed, then stepped around her. Skylar turned to see him slam his fist into the thing that had hurt her. As he went flying back, the man turned to her and smiled.

"You should go now. There is nothing here that you will remember. It was a cat." She looked at the creature now crawling toward them both, then at the man. "You will listen to me. Go into your home and to bed. You will remember nothing."

"I'm pretty sure that I'll remember a thing like that." She pointed to the creature, then looked at the man.

"You're really big, aren't you? I mean like freaky big. Do you work out or is it drugs that did this to you?"

"I have told you what to do, miss. Now run along." Skylar cocked a brow at him and crossed her arms over her chest. The man started to speak again, to no doubt spew some other ridiculous crap, but she kicked out at the creature just as he reached for the man's leg. "Go inside."

His voice thundered over her, and she smiled. There was something so...she supposed childish about the man. When he turned from her and grabbed the creature again, she watched in horror as he fought with it.

The thing was strong, and his mouthful of teeth seemed to come pretty close to the man's throat several times. But when he slammed his fist down his throat, gagging the thing until he stopped struggling, Skylar wasn't surprised to see him pull his heart out. When he turned to her, she knew as surely as he was standing there that he was going to eat it. But he tossed it away and walked toward her.

"Are you daft? Do you not have a single brain cell in your head? I have told you to go away. What part of that did you not understand?" She only stared at him. Skylar was afraid, but she had a feeling that he'd not hurt her. At least she hoped not. "What is wrong with you?"

"Nothing." There wasn't either. She felt really good. Wonderful, as a matter of fact. "I would ask you the same thing. What are you on and what was that thing? You killed it. I know it was going to kill me, but you killed it. By ripping his heart out."

"It is the only way to truly kill them where there is no...I asked you a question. Did you not understand when I told you to go inside?" She nodded and looked around. There were more of the creatures now, hundreds that she was sure was going to kill them both. "They will not harm us for now. They fear the same death as the one there. And why is it you can see them when other humans cannot."

"You're weird. Has anyone ever told you that before?" He took a step back when she poked him in the chest with her finger. "And I'm not a dog to be ordered to heel. You have something to ask me then ask, but you aren't my boss and I certainly am not afraid of your foul mood. Now back the fuck up and leave me alone."

When he backed up another step, she moved to go up the steps to her apartment. His low growl was all the warning she got before he lifted her up and pulled her to his body. He had his hand around her throat and held her to his body with her back to his chest.

"Do you know what I could do to you right now? I could take you, bend you over this railing, and fuck you until you are nearly dead. Then I could take your throat. Bite deeply into your pounding pulse and feed from you until you no longer exist." He bent her head to the left and licked along her throat. Instead of scaring her, which she was sure was his intention, it made her wet. Her body responded to him as if he were making love to her. "You are dangerous. Why are you here?"

His voice was low, sexy, and full of promise. When his mouth sealed over her throat, Skylar moaned. He was going to bite her. She had no idea why that sounded like the best thing in the world to happen to her, but when he lifted his head from her, she whimpered. Then she got pissed.

Fighting him caught him off guard, and he dropped her. She'd not realized how high on his body he'd held her until she fell to her knees. When he reached for her again,

Skylar came up with both her fists flying and hit him twice before he got both her hands. His mouth was bleeding when he pressed her against the wall of her building. He held her hands above her head.

"Stop this." Kicking out, she got him in the thigh. She tried to hit his groin. But he pressed his huge body against her and held her still with it. "Stop fighting me this instant. I do not want to hurt you."

Skylar slammed her head forward and hit him in the nose. He let her go and dropped to his knees. She was dropped again. This time she was prepared for it and as soon as her feet touched the ground, she took off. But it was a short-lived freedom as he grabbed her leg and pulled her back.

Kicking back at him, she connected with something soft and hard at the same time and heard him curse. But the harder she tried to get away from him, the stronger he seemed to get. When he was lying over her body, holding his head well out of reach for her, she lay there panting. Her wrists were in his one hand held above her head.

"I think I have made a mistake." Before she could tell him he was damned right, he continued. "I believe that you would have made short work of the monster that wanted you. Mayhap I will hire you to protect me next time."

"Get off me." But all he did was shift, and she felt his cock at her pussy. "Get off me please. You're too heavy."

"I think I am not." He rocked into her again, and she moaned. "You are very appealing when you are not spitting and fighting like a man. My poor nose is bruised. Do you not want to kiss it and make it better."

The thought of kissing him had her looking at his mouth. His low groan and him rocking into her pussy again had her curling her fingers around his hand holding her. Every part of her wanted him to do all sorts of things to her, and she was afraid that he'd be very good at it. Then what would she do when he left her?

"Let me up." He only continued to look at her mouth, and it took all her waning willpower to not lick her lips ready for him. "I'm finished fighting you. I just want up so that I can go into my home."

"I would very much like to sample you." A noise behind her had him looking away from her. Skylar felt as if she'd been robbed of something fantastic. "Our friends have decided that we've played long enough. If I let you rise, will you behave?"

"I'm going inside. You can or can't deal with whatever that thing was on your own." He looked at her for a long moment before he lifted his hard body from hers. His cock, thick and hard, was pressed so deep within her that Skylar was on the verge of begging him to let her taste him. "You will behave and answer my questions."

It wasn't a command so much as it was a statement. But her temper, never the best of things, was on red and she wanted to lash out at him again. Instead, she got up, ignoring the hand he had out for her and started for the door. He was right behind her.

"I'm going in. You, however, are not." He still followed behind her and when she got to the door, Skylar turned. "Look. I'm glad that you killed that thing, but there are a large number of them still here. I don't know what they are and right now, I really don't give a shit. I'm tired and I want to go inside."

"I shall go with you. You still have not answered me on how you are able to see the malefactors." Skylar looked at the creatures, then back at him. "You will tell me or I shall have to subdue you once again."

"What are they?" When he didn't answer, she looked at them. "They look like regular people, but I don't think they are. There is something…I guess you could call it 'blurry' about them. They're there, but they aren't quite solid. And they aren't in color. Grayed out and very pale."

"Malefactors. They are a group of 'soldiers,' for lack of a better term. I first encountered them many years ago on a battlefield. They came upon the dying and…one bite from them and you will become what they are. Men who served me, fought beside me, have been converted as well and are now, sadly, among them. The second generation cannot convert, but they do bring the dying that they'd bitten to a place where the others, the older ones can finish them off." He never took his eyes from hers as he continued. "They drain the blood of their victims before they eat their flesh. Bones and all. I have seen this so I know that it is true."

"Drain their blood like a vampire would." He nodded, then took a step closer to her. "You said that you wanted to bite me. Take my throat. Are you like them? Can you…do you have fangs as well."

"I do." He opened his mouth, and she took a step back. "I cannot change you. Had I been able to do that, I would not have been fighting this never-ending war by myself for so long. I am but a man."

"Hardly a man. Not with those things." She turned then and tried to press her key into the lock. It took her three tries until he finally took the keys from her and opened it for her. Before she opened the door to slip in, she turned back to him. "There are about a million questions running through my head right now. None of which have answers that I want to hear more than likely. Like, who are you and what are you doing here? Then there is the old man at the diner. What did he do to me and—Hey! What the hell are you doing?"

He tore her blouse up to her shoulder. All Skylar could do was stare at the marks there. They were red, bloodied red raw. It was like a tribal or something, but she couldn't tell what it was supposed to be. When he lifted her other arm up and tore her shirt sleeve up on that one, she was too afraid to fight him. There were marks on that arm as well, but these went from her shoulder to her wrist.

"Where did you see this man?" All she could do was stare at her arms. "Miss, you have to tell me. Where did you see him?"

"Where I work. He'd been in there a couple of times over the last few weeks. All he did was drink coffee and leave me a hefty tip. The first time...the tip caught me up on my rent. The second time...what is happening to me?" He opened the door behind her and when she staggered to move in, he picked her up in his arms. She found herself on her couch before she could think that she needed to be alone for a bit. "He did this to me? Is that what happened when he grabbed me?"

"Yes." The man disappeared to her kitchen and when he returned, he handed her a glass of water. "You have no spirits in your home that I could find."

"I don't drink." She downed the water and handed him back the glass. "Spirits? You know, I'll say this again, you're weird."

Skylar lay back on the couch. It wasn't a good couch, and she happened to be sitting on the least painful spring that came up from the cushions. The man sat on the chair only to rise up and glare at it.

"That is most uncomfortable." Skylar giggled, and he turned to look at her. "You are better now? I'd very much like to speak with you about this man. Did he tell you his name?"

"No. Never. And I only gave him coffee, not dated him." The man growled. "Now what? You know what, I don't care. As I've said, I'd like to think about what just happened. And I can't do that with you here. I appreciate you coming to help me after the fact, but I'm fine now and won't go near those things again."

"We are the same." She looked up at him and then at her arms. Pulling her tattered sleeve down, she shook her head. "The marks on your arm are the same as mine. There are a few that look like Davis's, but not all. Ours look to be the same all the way around. You will show me your back too."

"Stop ordering me around." Being pissed at him was easier than thinking about what had been done to her. "Go away. I want to take a shower and go to bed. I'm tired and I have to open the diner tomorrow by myself. Carly called off again. And who the hell knows where the owner is? He's not been around longer than he's been there. I'm thinking he's dead, or at least hoping so. Good thing the payroll is done by...why am I telling you all this?"

When she stood up, the man came toward her. Putting out her hand didn't stop him, not that she thought it would, but she had hoped that he'd get the hint. Apparently, he didn't take hints all that well, and she opened her mouth to tell him to get the fuck out of her life.

"I am Rembrandt, but I go by Remy. I am eighteen hundred and seventy-eight years old this year. When I was thirty-four, the man that touched you came to the battlefield where I was and told me he had a job for me." Remy pulled her body to his, and Skylar wrapped her arms around his shoulders. Her head was too busy sorting out what he was saying to have her body push him away. At least that was what she told herself. "He didn't mark me as he had you until recently. In all this time I have been alone. Killing the malefactors as best I could. I fed when I needed to, fucked when necessary, and I killed all the time. But right now, at this moment, all I can think about it taking you to bed. Fucking you until there are no more thoughts of dying or creatures."

He lifted her by her ass, and Skylar wrapped her legs around him. As he made his way to the bedroom, she pulled at the buttons on his shirt. As soon as she had it opened to where she could see his chest, Skylar buried her nose into his throat. She felt the shifting of her teeth even as she realized she needed to bite him.

His low growl of "do it" had her opening her mouth wide over his pounding pulse and sinking her teeth deep into his throat. The blood that filled her mouth had her wanting more even as the bed touched her back. Skylar was so fucked right now.

Chapter 3

Remy knew that her feeding from him was the best thing she needed. But he wanted more of her. All of her. Pulling at her clothing as she continued to drink from him, he tore at them rather than magically remove them from her body, as was his usual way.

He loved to undress a woman. See each part of her as he revealed it to himself. As he got to each morsel of a woman, he'd nip and taste her dewy skin, take his time with his exploration. But with this woman, he needed to fuck her. Now.

When he pulled her head back from his by tugging on her hair, he stood up and began to pull his own clothes off. She hurried to take the rags that were hers off, and he nearly fell atop her when she was naked. Christ, she was a goddess. He stood before her in only his pants and boots when she sat up.

"I want to see you." He nodded as she reached for his zipper. The snap had come off sometime when he'd been pulling at it, but now all he could think about was the woman before him. "I want to lick you as well. The thought of taking you into my mouth has me wet."

"Show me." She leaned back and spread her legs. "More, show me more of you. You're womanhood, open it for me."

Her fingers slid down her body to her furred entrance. As she pulled her nether lips open for him, Remy felt his cock grow harder. Pulling himself free was a necessity now or he'd hurt himself. Remy pulled his pants to his hips and stood over her, fisting his cock as she ran her finger over her swollen clit.

Dropping to his knees beside her bed, he watched her fingers play. He wanted to join them, slide his own into her sheath, and then drink from her. But Remy wanted to see her come, watch as her body hardened during her release, and then see her juices flow from her body. But the more he watched her, the harder his cock got, Remy knew that fucking this woman was going to be wondrous. Leaning into her, just to get her scent, he told himself, Remy licked her clit, then pulled it into his mouth and bit down.

She flooded his mouth. Her screams rang in his ears as she gave him her all. Remy drank and drank from her but still missed a good deal of her. When she cried out a second, then a third time, he knew that he had to have her. Standing up, he told her to go to the center of the bed. But she only shook her head.

"My turn." Giving him no time to tell her no, her mouth seemed to engulf him. Her hands were everywhere, and he had to hold onto the bed post or fall. She never stopped moving her fingers over his body, his balls, his ass, even the crown of his cock. When her mouth began a dance over him, bobbing up and down to the rhythm of his fucking her, Remy tightened his grip on the bed and reached for her head to pull her back from him. He wanted to come in her pussy.

But she shifted her body and swallowed him down past the tightness of her throat. Remy felt his balls twist in her hands, and suddenly she dug her nails into his ass. Remy felt his climax race along his entire body to explode out of the tip of his manhood into her mouth.

Remy fucked her luscious mouth hard. He knew that he had to be hurting her, but the thought of gentling his thrust, slowing for even a moment, had him fucking her harder still. When he was sure he could give her no more, she stood up and bent over the bed, her ass, a perfectly shaped heart, had his cock fill again, and he stepped behind her to slide his cock inside of her hot, wet pussy.

Remy grabbed onto her hips as he plowed her. Christ, he had never needed to come inside of a woman as he did her. Leaning over her, taking her head to the bed, Remy fucked her harder until his balls tightened up to his body. Bending over her, he offered her his wrist as he took hers to this mouth. And when he came, his cock once again erupting into her, he sank his fangs into her vein and drank greedily. Her bite had him growling around her wrist as she drank.

Remy rolled to his back when he thought the exertion wouldn't kill him. His heart was pounding so hard that he was sure that the entire neighborhood could hear it. Never had fucking a woman brought him so much pleasure.

"You need to leave now." Her voice was soft but hurt him in ways that he'd never had before. He'd had his wife, his love, hurt him like this once, and it had taken him weeks to get over it. But this time, unlike with his wife, he could find nothing that he'd done to her to warrant such a feeling.

"I should like to stay." She rolled off him and to the other side of the bed. He could see that the marks on her were bleeding still, and he wanted to pull her to him and lick them closed. But he didn't care for the look in her eyes. "You will not harm me, will you?"

"I want you to leave me alone. I don't know what this thing is, this sexual attraction between us, but we'll just have to get over it." When she stood up, he could see the markings were extended to her back. Before he could tell her so, she went into what he assumed was the bathroom and closed the door.

Remy got up. He still had his trousers but nothing else to pull on. He didn't bother zipping them up. Without the snap they would fall off anyway. Instead he pulled them as high on his hips as he could get them and wandered out to the kitchen area. He wasn't really looking for anything in particular when he came across some mail.

"Skylar Manning." Her name was beautiful, and he tasted it on his tongue several times by saying it over and over. But the words across the top of the bills made him frown. "Past Due," "Urgent," as well as a few other harsh demands. Opening the one that had yesterday's date on it, he was surprised at the amount that she owned on her credit card. Who would do something such as this?

"What do you think you're doing?" The letter demanding that she make more payments was suddenly gone from his hand. "You can't just go and read other people's mail. There are laws about that."

"I know your name now. Skylar Manning. And you owe a great deal of money to a lot of rude people." He thought she said something like "you have no idea" when she turned from him again. Her shirt was damp and he could see the blood seeping under the material. "I should heal you."

Standing, he pressed her into the counter and lifted her shirt up. The markers here were not words that he could see, but a design. She'd been marked with what looked like wings to him. But from the size, he knew that they'd never lift her from the ground. When he ran his tongue over the left one, holding her tightly as she struggled, he wasn't surprised when she stilled.

"Don't do that." He moaned when she pressed her ass back into him. Remy ran his hand up her thigh and under the shorts she hand on. Her panties were wet and very silky. "Stop. We're not having sex again."

Turning her in his arms after licking the other wing, Remy sat her on the counter. Pulling her pants off her, he looked down at the small silk that hid her womanhood from him. Putting his hands into the small strings at either side of her hips, he watched her face as he pulled the fabric hard enough to tear it from her.

Reaching into his open pants, she curled her fingers around his crown. Remy never took his eyes from her as he leaned forward and pulled her to him. His cock slid into her like a hand into a glove, and she closed her eyes.

"Look at me." Her eyes opened, and he stared into her. "You are hot, wet for me. My cock fits you like it should." He fucked her slowly, moving in and out of her. "I would taste your mouth now. Kiss you like lovers can and taste the dark richness of your mouth."

Her mouth moved under his, and Remy tasted the minty-ness of her mouth, the freshness of her shower. Gathering her closer to him, he lifted her up and pressed her against the wall to her right. Fucking her harder, he buried his mouth in her throat, again tasting her flesh as if for the first time. Scraping his fangs over the pounding pulse, he lifted his head and looked into her face.

"I want to bite you again." Nodding, Remy leaned his head to the side to give it to her. But she only stared at him, not taking what he freely offered. "Why am I not grossed out about doing this? Why am I not terrified of you fucking me without protection? And those things out there? Why am I not scared shitless of them?"

"I know not." He saw the tears then, filling her eyes until they spilled out. "Come for me. Bite me and feed deeply. We will work this out when we are sated."

"We're never going to be satisfied, I think." Before he could tell her she might be right, her mouth was at his throat again. And when she bit him, his cock exploded inside of her and he bit into her wrist, taking as much of her into him as he could. Her own release took his breath away in its beauty.

~~~

The shower Skylar took this time was more to work out the soreness than to scrub his scent off her. She should have known that he'd still be here when she got out. Not even telling him she was going to call the police if he was here seemed to faze him. At least this time he wasn't going through her mail but sitting on her couch and seemingly waiting for her. He stood up when she entered the room. Christ, she should have given him a towel to put over his chest. Or a blanket would have been better, the more he covered the better.

"We need to have a conversation. I know that you have many questions, but I don't have all the answers." Skylar sat on the floor. It was more comfortable than any of her furniture anyway. She noticed that he had gotten her pillows from her bed and was sitting on them. He offered the plush area to her.

"No thanks, and don't get too comfortable either. You're leaving when I'm satisfied." Her words, innocently spoken brought a smile to his face and heat to her body. "I meant with my questions."

"I should like to take you back to the bedroom and make love to you again and again until your questions, large or small, mean very little to you." She knew that he could too and that was the problem. "But you are correct. We need to figure this out. As for your questions, as I have said, I don't know how much I can answer you."

"What was that man? I'm assuming, and this is really concerning me because I'm not afraid of you or him, that he's like you are." He nodded, then shook his head. "So he's different than you are?"

"I believe that you are like us as well. At least like me." He stood up and showed her his arms. "We are the same, marked alike. Another man, Davis Brown, has recently met with this man too, a man in black with a cane, and he too is marked. But his are different than ours."

"What are these marks?" He told her he didn't know. "Then why the hell do we have them? Why is having sex with you all I can think about? And when the fuck did I get fangs to bite you like I do?"

Her body tensed up when he came toward her. But instead of touching her, he only sat beside her. Pulling her arm to his, she could see that not only did their markings seemed to be the same, but when they were touching like they were now, she could feel a heat, a tremendous amount of energy come from them.

"This mark, what do you know of it?" She told him nothing. "Watch this. I don't... When we were together, I brushed my mark against this one. Like this."

Remy lifted her up and sat her on his lap so that her back was to his chest. When he lifted her arm with his left one and pressed his left one to hers from beneath, she felt the heat again, and her body felt...

"I feel fantastic." He groaned when she moved over his hips. "Stronger too. Like I could lift a car. And that I could...I could fly."

"I believe that you can." She turned and looked at him to see if he was making fun of her. But he pulled his arm from hers. And while she was still energized, she wasn't as strong as she had been. "We are matched somehow. When fighting, I think should we fight side by side, we will be stronger still."

"Fight?" He nodded and helped her off his lap. Skylar felt cooler still but let it go in favor of finding out what was going on. "I'm not going to fight those things out there. I don't know what they are, but I don't have the strength to do that stuff. Besides, I need my paying job. I'm sure you noticed that I'm a little behind in my life. And I have a feeling that what you're talking about doesn't pay."

"It does. Very well. I have a great deal of my pay saved and we, Davis and I, are looking to find a place where we can live. All of us." She was shaking her head. "You will need to be with us now, Skylar. You are no longer safe alone here. They will hunt you as you will need to hunt them."

"What are you?" He only sat there. "I'm so overwhelmed right now. I don't even know where to begin. Why did you have sex with me? It had to be more than just an itch."

"Itch? If you mean that I needed sex, then you are partially correct. I did. But not what you are thinking. I needed to drink from you, fuck you. No one else, not in all my lifetime has anyone satisfied me as you have done."

"You never…you don't have to flatter me. I get it was great sex, but come on." He grinned at her and rubbed his hand over his hard cock. "You can't want me again. I mean, Christ, we just had major sex three times."

"I want you over me right now. Riding my cock as I suckle at your nipples. I wish to watch your face as you reach your peak, take my pleasure while you are in the thralls of your own. Come here, Skylar, let me show you just how much I would like to have you again."

Standing up, she walked to him. His mouth was right where he could eat her, and the thought of his mouth over her again had her shifting on her feet. But when he pulled her pants down to her knees, he didn't eat her, but slid his finger into her and pressed his thumb over her clit.

"Please, I thought I was going to ride you." He moved closer to her, his mouth just inches from her clit. "Eat me. I need to come."

"I want to drink you here." Skylar felt as if he had already bitten her and was right now feeding from her. "You're soaking my hand. Your juices are dripping down my arm. I'm going to enjoy this."

His mouth moved over her, and his tongue curled around her clit several times before he finally sucked it into this mouth. Skylar held onto his head, holding him there or simply holding on. She didn't know, but she knew that he couldn't stop until she came. But when he bit her, his fangs sinking deep into her clit, she screamed out her release. And even as he sucked harder, taking more of her blood into him, she came again, then a third time before she felt her knees weaken from it.

"Come here." Remy pulled her down over him. His touch was urgent but firm. Before she could figure out what he wanted, she was impaled on his cock and riding him. "Christ, give them to me. Let me have your breasts."

Skylar tore open her shirt; her bra followed the torn clothing to the floor as she pulled his head to her left then right breast. He bit her each time, leaving the wound open as he nursed from her. All the while his cock was filling her, her hips were moving over him at a speed she'd never thought of herself as having. When he told her to bite him, drink from him, Skylar leaned forward even while he continued to suckle at her, and bit deeply into his shoulder. She screamed again around his flesh as blood filled her mouth and body. She came so hard that darkness seemed to run over her.

When she woke, she was in her bed. Naked but covered with her comforter. Looking around for Remy, she was both disappointed and relieved to see him gone. Lying back on the pillow, she thought about all the he'd done to her and her to him. When she heard the bathroom door open, she looked over at him and felt her body respond to his nudity.

"We must speak." Nodding, she watched him pull on a pair of silk boxers and then a pair of leather pants. As he sat in the chair next to the bed and pulled on his boots, all she could think of was how many times she'd come with this man. And how incredibly stupid she'd been for doing it.

"You're leaving." He nodded, then shook his head. "You know, you do that a lot. Tell me yes then shake your head no. Are you leaving here or not?"

"I am. But you are as well." She shook her head, and he nodded again. "You must come with me. I have to look at a building for us to live in and I would appreciate your opinion. In the event there are others out there like you."

It went straight to her heart. She had no idea that words, such meaningless words by themselves, alone could cause so much pain. Instead of answering him, of giving him any sort of clue as to her pain, she got up and went to the bathroom. She turned on the shower and reached to lock the door when it flew open.

"You will come with me. There are malefactors all around this building now. They will find you here alone and kill you. I cannot have that happen. You will—"

"You will not order me around." It occurred to her that she was naked, but her temper got the better of her. "If you want to go out and find another fuck buddy, be my guest, but I will not help you pick out your bedroom suite so the little woman is happy."

"What are you talking about?" Not answering him, she shoved him back and stood there for several seconds when he landed across the room from her and into the living room. But gathering her wits when he started to stand, she slammed the door and locked it to her bedroom. "Open this door please. I should like to get this matter cleared up before we go."

Skylar stepped into the warm water. As it rained over her head, she let the tears fall. What the hell was wrong with her? She never had sex with strangers. It wasn't like her to let a man hurt her either, and here she'd done both. Reaching over her head, she pulled down her shampoo and nearly dropped it when one of the creatures appeared beside her. Instead of screaming and having the dick on the other side break the door down, which she had no doubt that he'd do, she slammed her fist into his mouth and down his throat and found his heart. Pulling it out, she stood there with it still beating in her hand when Remy broke the door down and threw back the shower curtain.

"He was just there." Remy nodded and pushed her under the water. The heart was cold and no longer beating, but Remy took it away. He handed her the sponge from the shelf and squirted nearly half the bottle of soap onto it. Then when he pressed it to her body, she began scrubbing herself as hard as she could. Remy told her to turn her back to what he was doing.

Skylar had never concentrated so hard on her bath in her life. There were noises behind her, things going on that she didn't want to know. And when the water was turned off and a towel handed to her, she took it and began drying.

"You will not argue with me now." Shaking her head, she decided that living alone wasn't going to be the same again. "I have packed you a bag. And on the counter there are clothes for you to put on. When I return I—"

"Don't leave me." He nodded toward the bloodied sheet on the floor. "Oh. I see. But you'll come back? You won't...I'll do whatever you need for your girlfriend or whatever she is. Just don't leave me here with those things."

"I won't." He moved out of the bedroom with the sheet draped thing over his shoulder. Skylar grabbed her clothing and went into her bedroom where a piece of luggage she'd never seen before was laying open on her bed. And in it were her things. Dressing as quickly as she could, Skylar got her hair brush from the dresser and sat on the bed. Counting the strokes to her hair, she thought about all the things she might be leaving behind and was all right with that. Nothing in the bathroom was leaving with her, she was sure of that.

When he returned, he was dressed in clean clothes. There wasn't any blood on him either. When he reached for the bag, he looked at her before pulling her into his arms and holding her. Then with a kiss on the forehead, he took her hand and led her out of the apartment. As soon as they reached the sidewalk, he buried her face in his chest and took her to a waiting car. In seconds, they were moving down the road.

Chapter 4

The building was huge. Remy looked at Davis, then back at the warehouse he'd told him to meet him at. There were malefactors all around the place, but none of them were going inside. Skylar was standing as far from him and Davis as she could get.

"We have to go and fight them. Mark this place." Remy nodded, knowing that he was right but having no idea how to go about it. "If we don't, they'll come and go as they please. Taking one of us with them."

"I know." He glanced at Skylar, then at the building. "Do you have any idea how to do that? I mean, I can see where you are correct, but having the knowledge is not there for me."

"With the marks on our bodies." They both looked at Skylar when she spoke. "These will protect us. I'm betting that. How? I have no clue, but I can't think that whoever this asshole is that marked us is going to let me be killed right off the bat. There is something there, don't you think?"

"Which ones?" She glared at him, and he had to smile. "I only ask because you and I are marked well. Davis has some, but not as you and I do. And he has no wings."

Remy had been surprised to know that he'd had some as well. His were bigger but not nearly big enough to carry his weight. Then there were the marks on his legs. Those frightened him enough that he wasn't able to ask either Skylar or Davis if they had them as well. They were guns. Large and frighteningly efficient-looking guns.

"Do I have to think of everything?" When she stomped to the building, he nearly followed her. But Davis put his hand on his chest and told him to wait. "We just have to figure out which ones scare the shit out of them."

They surrounded her almost immediately. Once she reached out and killed one of them, shoving her hand down his throat and pulling out his heart as he'd done today, he had to grip the hood of the car. She was fearless or stupid. Remy was afraid that she was a good deal of both. Once she dropped the body and heart, a few of them scattered, but as soon as she pulled the long sleeved shirt off she'd pulled on, all of them gave her a wide berth.

"Something on this arm." It just happened to be the arm that was covered from top to bottom. It was, as far as he could see, about as useless as not knowing anything. But before he could voice his opinion on her lack of help, the man in black appeared before him.

"She is a good deal smarter than I had first thought." The guns at his hips burned, and he put his hand on the one on his left hip. "Do not attempt to harm me, Rembrandt. It will only serve to upset me, and I've no reason as yet to cause you harm." When the man stiffened and put up his hands, Remy had a moment of fear. It was magic, he thought, but when Skylar spoke behind the man, Remy smiled.

"You know Skylar, don't you? She was leaving work when you touched her. What did you do to her besides put her into harm's way?" The man said nothing. "I don't know what she's doing to you to have the look of fear on your face, but I would heed what she tells you. In our short acquaintance, I have discovered that she can be vicious."

"She is your reward." The man winced and took an involuntary step in his direction. That was when Remy saw the blade in Skylar's hand and that she was holding it on the man. It was deep within the jacket that the man had on, and Remy had a feeling it was pricking his skin. "I have explained to you that a reward was coming to you. It is her."

When he turned to look at Skylar, so did Remy. He'd seen that look before. Hurt, pain, and a little anger. But he had a feeling that her pain was winning out, and he moved to take her into his arms. But she backed from them both.

"Don't touch me." Remy nodded but didn't move back. When she looked at the man in black, Remy had a moment of fear. Not for him but the other man. "What the fuck do you mean, I'm his reward? You don't just go around giving a person as a reward. And what the fuck is this shit on me? Take it off. Right now."

"I cannot. And even if I could, I would not. You are his to help him. A reward is a bad choice of wording." She backed up again, and Remy wanted to pull her back. But he also knew that touching her now would get them both hurt. "I should like to explain."

"I don't give two farts in the wind what you have to say now. Take this shit off me. Right fucking now." The man stepped back, and Skylar took two toward him. "Then I'll kill you."

The man reached out and no doubt meant to stop Skylar from harming him. But the moment was lost when five of the malefactors came toward them. Remy reached for Skylar, but she sidestepped him and killed the creature closest to her before he could protect her. Then it was everything he could do to keep himself from being harmed.

The man fought with them. Davis was knocked down minutes into the fight, and his left arm disappeared in the melee. He didn't know if it was bitten off or a mislaid sword caught him. Standing up, he staggered twice before he was helped to the car by Skylar. She managed to knock one of the bad guys at him to protect them just as she shoved Davis in the car. He was reasonably safe for now, and she came to him and fought beside him.

It was over in minutes. It had seemed longer than it was to him because he had so much fear that Skylar would have been hurt. But twice she'd saved him simply because he was too focused on her to keep himself safe. As they moved away from the bodies, he pulled her to him and glared at the man.

"Your name." The man shook his head, and Remy pulled his gun out. It was useless in this fight, but it might hurt the man. "Tell me your name or I end our relationship now. I am surely sick of your face."

He looked at the bodies and then at them. There were more than he'd thought, over a dozen of them laying there with their chest split open in some cases but all of them without their hearts. There was something else he noticed too. Two of them were not malefactors. He looked at the man again.

"They are not." Remy knew the man read his mind. He'd been doing it from the start. He didn't like it, but he knew that telling the man to stop would be akin to telling Skylar to stay where it was safe. "She is your helpmate. You and she together are the most...you are powerful beyond compare."

Remy moved closer to the downed creatures. When he looked up at the ones around the building, he realized that more of them were malefactors than not, but there were a great many of the newer creatures. These were faded so deeply that they were almost translucent. Skylar bent over them as well and touched one of the new creatures with the tip of the knife she had in her hand. Remy watched her as the man in black spoke.

"I thought they were only first and second generation, but I don't know now. The second ones are...faded. These are more than that. I had thought, well, I thought that it was impossible for new ones to convert, but I was wrong. The war has gotten that much harder if these are a third group." Skylar looked at him, then at the man as he continued. "There will be more of them than we first thought."

"You want the three of us to fight them?" The man looked at him, and Remy decided he was on his own. "What the fuck are we supposed to do? Piss on them and hope that kills them off quickly? Or did you have some sort of bomb in your pocket you were going to surprise us with?"

"I have no bomb. And I have taken the liberty of bringing on more men and women for you to work with as I have told you before. There will be twelve of you when it is all finished. And the work you will accomplish will make it so that mankind will not be turned into a savage." Skylar stood up and the man took a step back. "You will not harm me, Skylar Manning. It is not within your nature to—"

Her fist caught the man square in the nose. As he staggered back, Skylar advanced on him. Remy caught her around the waist when it looked like she was going to pounce on the man once again. He held her up so that she didn't take her anger out on him. But Remy had to smile. She was a good warrior.

When she noticed something on her hand, she stilled. He didn't see it but whatever it was had the man backing from her. His fervent *no* had Remy thinking that she'd pulled some sort of weapon on him, but she only licked her knuckles. The two-way connection between him and Skylar expanded to the man as well.

"I know his name. I know everything about him." Remy put Skylar down as the creatures around them gathered closer. He knew that there were rumors about knowing a person's name was akin to having their heart in your hand, but now he knew it to be true. Skylar was cut off from speaking again when the man stood up.

"Giving them my name will give them powers over all of us." Skylar nodded but said nothing. "You should be put to death for what you've done to me. No one is to touch me. Not ever."

"Yet I did." She stood up to the man, and Remy felt his pride in her double. She was his reward. Not that he'd ever call her that again, but knowing that she was not exactly what the man was hoping for when he chose her for him made him very happy. "You weren't going to help us. Even with all your riches and powers, you were going to simply let us do this while you sat back and took the glory for it."

"I have helped, have I not? I brought the two of you together. And at great expense of power I have also brought the others to you. They will arrive one at a time as you are getting prepared. You should never...I would like it if you never told others of the newcomers. It will be better for all if you kept their names to yourself." Skylar shook her head. "You think to do this on your own? You will surely die."

"No, what you're going to do is set up this building for us. Rooms with baths, beds, and whatever else is needed to make the incoming people comfortable. And you're going to mark this place and however much more surrounding area that we need that is a safe haven for them. A kitchen with someone to cook as well as a medical staff on duty at all —"

"I will not." Skylar took another step toward the man, and Remy followed. When she slid her arm to his, their marks met and he felt the power race over them. "Christ. You have more than we...you are not what I wanted in a reward. I had hoped that you'd keep him safe, work with him...you are going to be harder to control than we first thought."

He said it now as if he had meant to insult her. But Skylar only smiled at him, and Remy had a feeling that had he not held her back, she would have hurt him again. When the man only stood still and glared, Remy wondered why he didn't run.

"Have you no clue as to your powers, Rembrandt? Yours and hers?" He shook his head at the man. "She has figured out that she can hold a being. I know not how she has done it, but I cannot move. And if any of my other members were to come to help me, they too would be held. She is most strong. And you are helping her. Not at all very grateful of you, Rembrandt."

"I'm not grateful to you at all. Except for bringing her into my life." Remy let his fangs show, and he nuzzled into her shoulder. When she offered him her throat, he bit her gently and then looked up at the man when he sealed the wound. "You didn't expect that either, did you? That she would fulfill me in ways nothing else had."

"She was to be your bed partner and a person for you to vent upon. To feed you when it was inconvenient for you to leave. I was to give her a mark so that you'd keep her close, but whatever else she got was not from me." He looked angry. "The others will not be happy about this. I should not even tell them. I will simply…there are things going on that should be kept safe for now. You will keep her safe by not letting the others know."

When Skylar looked at the building, he did as well. There were changes going on. Most of them cosmetic, but he could see that there were also structural ones happening as well. The walls seemed to expand and stretch in height. The roof, a sad sort of looking thing, became a hard surface, metal he supposed. The windows that had been broken were now replaced with new bigger ones. And he could see that some art was happening as well.

As he watched, markings were drawn onto the grounds surrounding it. Hieroglyphics like the one on their bodies. As they stood there watching the transformation happen, Davis got out of the car whole again.

"It just appeared. My arm that they took off, it was just there." Remy nodded, words failing him. As Davis put out his hand to shake, Remy took it and felt the strength that wasn't there before. The two of them waited with Skylar as the building began to look like an oversized home and not the broken down warehouse it had been. He wondered what the hell had changed the man's mind and had him helping now.

~~~

Hector watched the building, as did the rest of them. All they knew him by was "the man in black," which suited him, he supposed. Until now. The girl had taken his blood. Something he'd never thought would happen. When another of his kind appeared beside him, he only glanced his way and then looked back at the building. Hector let his body fade to the other realm while he talked to his colleague.

"Do you suppose Rembrandt understands that he's the one that is making this?" Hector only shrugged at Dolin. He would not tell him that it was the two of them, not just Rembrandt. "What did you do to him?"

"Nothing. Other than what I was told, nothing at all. And when they're together, they are stronger than we first thought, but not by much. They will be easy to control when we need them." Dolin only nodded at his lie. Hector didn't know why it was important that she remained a secret as well as the power of Rembrandt. "Did you? Did you know what he would gain from this?"

"I had a thought that they'd be strong together, but I was hoping for them to be weaker, I suppose. I believe...I know that the two of them will do more in one year than we can do on our own in a century. They will be able to control the malefactors." Hector thought so as well. "We must talk to them. I will need to show them how to use their bodies now."

"I think it will be a mistake." Dolin asked him why. "They have more control over this than I had thought. He is making a place for them to stay, a 'safe haven,' she called it. I believe if we tell them what they have with this, they will overuse their powers in ways that will harm even us."

"I do not think so, but you are with them. I would think they'd be grateful for what they've gained. But as I have said, you know them better than me." Hector had seen such power go to a human's head. Not any power that these two had but enough that it nearly destroyed mankind. It was why he had chosen Rembrandt. He'd had nothing. "When will you talk to them? I should like to be there if only in the shadows."

"Soon. But they will need help, I think. A few men. Do you have any in mind? I have one or two. This man Davis and Nathaniel Livingston. The only one that I worry about is Nathaniel. He is… Nathaniel has had some things go sour in his life that has made him bitter. I worry that he will need to be destroyed and replaced. He will be…at the rate they are moving here, he will be the last to arrive. I hope it will not be too late."

Dolin only nodded. Hector knew things that this man did not. Some of them he supposed he should share but a great deal of them he would not. It was his responsibility to keep this group safe and working. The malefactors, as Rembrandt called them, were getting stronger daily. But he was concerned over his partner. He didn't wholly trust him of late.

"We should never have invented them to have a mind of their own." Hector looked at Dolin. "It is the greatest mistake we made. I wish daily that we had simply walked away. But now...there are more of them coming. Too many, I fear, for this group to conquer."

"We had thought they'd be like Rembrandt. A warrior to help fight wars." Hector hated to admit it, even to himself but he'd been partly responsible for the malefactors on this realm. Dolin had convinced him that it would work for this world. They had worked so well for them on theirs that they had rewarded them by sending them here. But they'd given them no restrictions. None at all, and within a few years, they had turned to rogues. Murdering rogues that had no qualms about killing anything and everyone.

"We will need to work faster." Hector looked at Dolin. "They spread now. Far beyond where we are now, there are a few that are working to start another faction."

"I can destroy that, but this many will be hard to hide." Hector made a mental note to talk to Rembrandt without the girl. She was just too knowing of him. There were things he did not what her to know. But he feared that she may already be privy to his deepest, darkest secrets. "I will talk to them soon. Their home is nearly complete. Soon they will enter and I will tell them to ward against us, even our kind to go into their perimeter."

"Why?" Then it occurred to Dolin. "We are the same as the malefactors. If we can enter, so might they. Good thinking. I am glad that you are in charge and not me. But I must leave. They will do well, Hector, you will see."

As soon as Dolin left him, Hector moved into the realm where the humans were. The way that Rembrandt was looking at him made him think that the warrior knew something, but he only nodded as they moved within the perimeter. Hector waited for him to turn back.

"I cannot enter." Rembrandt looked at where he stood, then back at him. "The hold that keeps you safe also keeps me from entering. And to change that will leave you exposed. I cannot do that. All that enter here will be safe from everything."

Which was true. Without Rembrandt or Skylar letting him cross the line, he was going to be on the outside. If the man had a clue that he was like the ones he fought, he didn't say anything. His nod only left Hector feeling a little relieved. But he knew that it would be short-lived. The man was very smart and would figure it out sooner rather than later.

Hector moved from this realm to his own to think. The girl having his blood would prove to be his downfall, and Hector wasn't sure how he felt about that. If she knew she was well within her rights to kill him, and he would be beheaded. If she told Dolin, or any of the others, he would be beheaded. He was a dead man either way.

Hector had been the last to leave the lab that day. He had wanted to put only a drop of his blood in one vial. Just on a lark, he had told himself. But it had been more than that. It had been a way to show them, the others in the lab, that he knew more than they did.

What had happened had been disastrous. Instead of a drop, he'd ended up putting three drops of his powerful blood in about a dozen of the vials. Showing off, he knew now. But his mistake had been, well, one of them had been that he'd not marked them. Not seen to it that they could be pulled if necessary. And when all but a dozen test subjects had died, the other's bodies simply not strong enough to take the weaker blood into their systems, Hector knew it was his blood that had changed them.

These beings, some of their kind that they had used for wars against other realms, had known from the start that they were test subjects, but it still hurt him when those others hadn't made it. And it might have worked had they left them here on their realm rather than sending them out to help others. Earth had not been a good project.

From the first, they were not what they had had in their realm. Death and mayhem had followed them everywhere they had gone. Of the dozen that were made, they had made more of his mistake and put it into hundreds, nay, thousands of humans. A single bite, they had discovered too late, to a human would make them what they were. And the five hundred subjects that had ended up on earth had changed to five million in no time.

Hector and a few others had killed a great many of them. Going from place to place that they had left them to destroy their creations. As well as their offspring. But some had slipped away. Some of them had gotten past them and now they were many again. Wars, not like they had had when Rembrandt was converted, would not be able to cover what they had now.

Changing Rembrandt had been risky. He was a good man, a lost man without any attachments. His skill as a hunter first for his family then as a warrior in the wars had had him win out over all the other men they had been watching. And Rembrandt had proven to them that there were still good people on earth. His work had kept Hector from giving up and simply letting the malefactors do what they would. There were more good than bad, and to him there were a great many bad people.

As he entered into his room, he looked at his sleeping child first. He was the light of his life, the joy that he needed daily to go on. But the child was sick, dying. Hector leaned down and kissed his brow and covered him with a blanket. He looked up when the nurse, Mary, who also acted as their housekeeper, cleared her throat.

"He has had a good day, sire." Hector nodded. "Do you think that the people there, the ones on earth, will help him? I surely hope so."

"I don't know, Mary, I just don't know." He looked at the bedroom beyond and then at his son. "Has there been any change to my wife?"

"No, my lord." He had hoped but knew that there would never be. She was simply too far gone now. Too ill for even him to heal. When the nurse left him, Hector sat on the chair and looked at his son. He too would die from the illness that his wife had succumbed to as well. It was his punishment, he knew, for what he'd done all those centuries ago.

Chapter 5

Remy walked around the building. There was so much more than he'd been able to imagine. Room after room of space. And some of it was filled already. When Skylar walked by the room he was in, he called her to him. She stood in the doorway and didn't come in as he'd hoped, but for now he'd let her shy away.

"What room would you call this one?" She looked around, then back at him. He had never seen so much equipment in his life, all of it humming with power. "I know that these are computers, but what use do we have of so many?"

"I would say that each person that lives here can work at them. There are things you'd have to research as well, correct?" He nodded and she backed away from the door. "I have to go to work in an hour. I missed yesterday, and I can't miss another day."

"What do you mean?" He moved toward the door to stop her should she try to leave. "You've taken on the job here. I need you."

"You asked me to look at a house for you and some woman. I did. It's nice and I'm sure that she'll love it." It took Remy a few moments to think what woman she was referring to, and when he remembered their conversation, she was already down the stairs. Shouting for her did no good, as she was not slowing in her haste to leave him.

At the bottom of the stairs, she was talking to Davis. The man was forever talking to her, and Remy hated it. No, that wasn't it. He didn't hate it, but it bothered him more than he thought it should. When she turned after Davis left, he pulled her into the room closest to them and shut the door. The fire in her eyes made his cock swell with need.

"I do not have a woman to come here. I only have you." The foot tapping and her arms across her chest had him trying to think what he'd said wrong now. "I want you to live here with me. As my partner. Sleep with me, work with me."

"Why?" Remy was startled by the question, but before he could think of an answer, she was talking again. And pacing. He so loved watching her pace. Her breasts did the most amazing things when she did that. But when she stopped moving and looked at him, he had a feeling he'd missed something important.

"I want you." She only glared harder. "I do. My cock to be buried inside of you is all I can think about."

"Sex is all you ever think about." It was true, but he didn't agree with her. There was something absolutely terrifying about her look right now. "I need more than just a roll in the hay with you. I need to feel like I'm a part of this relationship. I enjoy you fucking me, but that's all we do, fuck."

"I don't understand that statement." She huffed and turned from him. When he touched her, stopped her from leaving him, she turned so quickly that he backed up. She was upset. More than that, she was pissed off. "What did I do?"

"Nothing." He was standing there alone trying to think what he'd done to have her so upset and leaving him when Davis came into the hallway. He looked at him, and the man smiled.

"You and the missus having problems?" Remy nodded, not correcting him on the assumption that they were wed. "She's a right pistol, that one. I would say that happens when they don't know which way is up."

"Riddles. I don't understand you any more than I do her. She said that all I did was fuck her. She admitted to liking it, but she seemed upset." Davis smiled bigger and laughed. "This is not at all funny. She's upset and now she's going to work. I don't want her to go to work. Unless it's for me. Here in this house."

"You don't want a lot of things, I'm thinking." Before he could tell the man he wasn't helping, Davis continued. "She's not sure where she stands with you. Bed partner or a partner. Do you want her only for the sex, which is what she means by fucking, or do you want her companionship? There is a difference."

"My wife was never this complicated." He hadn't thought of his wife in days, not since meeting Skylar. "She was soft and bidding. Whenever I needed something or had a thought, she was one step ahead of me. Food…we would have dinner together and she took care of me. I don't know what to do with Skylar."

"I can see that." Remy growled, and Davis laughed again. "Do you love her? Or do you only keep her around so that you can get a quick, easy fuck and a meal?"

Remy was shocked by the question. An easy fuck? What did that even mean? He saw to her needs before his own. And he was sure that she was far from a meal. There was something about her that made him want to —

"She was my reward." Davis laughed again, this time making Remy so mad that he felt like hitting him. Instead, he only watched as he walked away. People were doing that to him a great deal lately, and he didn't care for it. Going outside, he watched as the malefactors surrounded the compound.

He went only to the edge of where they stood. Two of them, braver ones he supposed, moved a foot over the barrier and screamed out in pain. As they fell back, Remy moved closer and let several more of them die before he felt better. But the feeling soon disappeared with his mood.

It was them or him. He had felt that way for so long that he knew that it was true. Even before he'd had a few humans help him, and Remy had long since stopped thinking of himself as a human, he still was alone in this war. But lately, just lately, he was beginning to feel like he had someone to talk to. Skylar. And as he stood there watching the creatures, he noticed something else about them. They all looked exactly alike.

Never before had he had time to observe them. It was kill or be hurt. And he could get hurt from them. Looking down at the scar that still frightened him a little, he remembered the day he'd gotten it. The first day on the job as a warrior.

The malefactor had come upon him when he'd been on his way to his home. He'd had enough. His body was healed thanks to the touch of the man in black, and he wanted to begin his life anew. Even without the love of his life and his children, Remy knew that there had to be more to life than just killing. As he entered his home, small and dark as it was, he knew a terror that he'd never felt before. The malefactor was eating a man he'd killed. Remy had been stunned to stupidity. He knew that now.

And this one spoke to him. "You are dead. Or you should be. What have you done, human? Who has breached our promise?"

"Promise?" The creature nodded. "I don't know what you speak of. I am here to begin my life. I have no quarrel with you."

"But you do. You were made to kill me. And my offspring." He dropped the leg he'd been chewing on. "What will you do now, warrior? You are a warrior, are you not? Do you have what it takes to kill a...I am not armed."

He'd taken two steps to him, and Remy had felt the coldness of his body as he got closer. He didn't want to kill him, but he would not die either. Not by this creature's hands. When he touched him, burned his coldness deep into his body, Remy cried out and fell to the floor. The pain in his arm was there even after all these years. The handprint of their encounter a constant reminder of what he'd done.

The being had attacked him, came at him while Remy had been suffering through the pain. He'd only just managed to ram his hand down his throat in an effort to keep him from biting him. He had never understood why the thing had not bitten him then, but none since had either. Once he touched his heart, felt his beating in his hand, Remy knew a strength that he'd never had before and pulled it from his chest. The heart lay in his palm as the creature crumpled to the floor.

"Remy?" He turned, his entire body still in the past while his mind tried to work to understand what the man next to him was saying. Davis stood very still as he continued. "Are you okay? There's a phone call for you. Miss Skylar. She said for you to get your ass down at the diner right now. And not to forget to bring me with you. I think she's in a bit of trouble."

Remy ran to the car. Davis was right beside him when he opened the door and got in. He was peeling out of the drive when he released he had no idea where he was going. Davis, thankfully, did.

"I could hear some screaming. Like them monsters. I think she's got her more than she can handle." Remy felt his heart racing at the thought of something happening to her. "Calm as a baby she was, just said to me to bring you along if you weren't too busy and that if you was coming to hurry it up a bit. Damn, but I love that woman."

Remy nearly drove the car off the road. Christ, he loved her as well. But he knew that wasn't possible. He still loved his wife. It took them ten minutes to get there, breaking all sorts of laws on the way. He wondered briefly what the fine was for running five stop lights and going more than double the posted speed through the little town. When he pulled up in front of the place, simply called Diner, the entire building was ablaze.

He nearly knocked Davis down when he tried to stop him from going in. But he told him several times he thought, that he could see her. And that she was all right. When Remy finally saw her, covered in blood and soot, he dropped to his knees. She was all right, nothing had happened to her. As soon as she came toward him, Remy could see that blood was not just the malefactor's, some of it was hers as well.

"I'm all right." He didn't wait for her to say anything else but pulled her to his mouth and kissed her. When he lifted his head, looking down at her battered and bruised face, he could see her fear and something else. She looked like she was happy to see him.

~~~

"They were waiting for me." Skylar shivered when she told the cop what had happened. Remy was beside her still having told the officer that he wasn't leaving no matter what. The cop had looked at him for several seconds before he nodded. There was something incredibly sexy about a man in charge, she realized. "I walked in after unlocking the door, and I was jumped. They knocked me to the floor, then started beating on me."

"And you think they'd been there to rob the place." She nodded. That wasn't why they were there, and she was pretty sure that Remy knew it as well. So far as she could tell, she'd told the cop, nothing was missing. "Did you get a look at any of them? Or to see how many there were?"

She knew how many she'd killed. But if any got away, there was no way for her to know. It had been scary there for a while, and she'd only just managed to call the house when she'd locked herself in the kitchen. That was something else she'd have to ask about. Did they know that the creatures could slide under doors by shifting to a heavy cloud?

When he repeated his question to her, she shook her head. "I was too busy trying to curl into a ball. They were kicking and hitting me. I just wanted it over."

Again, not entirely true. She'd been the one kicking and hitting. They had been so stunned by her actions that she'd managed to kill two before they realized that she could hurt them. Then the fight had gotten nasty. And a good deal more than she'd been ready for.

Skylar supposed she should have been paying attention to her surroundings. But she was still hurt by the whole house thing. She loved it. It was what she might have picked out for herself. And now some other woman was going to live there. And Skylar had been pissed.

"Miss Manning, is there anything else you can tell us?" She shook her head. "We're trying to get in touch with the manager now. It seems that the number you gave us has been disconnected."

"I know. I've been trying to call him for a week now. I was just hoping that you'd have another way of reaching him once you found out that didn't work." He told her that he'd look into it. "When you talk to him, tell him that he no longer has to worry about the electric being disconnected. I think that's covered too. And there isn't enough money in the bank to cover my check. I just got informed as I was leaving my house that the last three checks they've written for me have bounced. I don't make much, but that's going to hurt me when the bounced check charges start rolling in."

After the cop left her sitting on the bench across from the building, she looked at her place of employment. Gone. Everything in it was gone. And if she didn't miss her bet, she'd bet the buildings on either side were about to go as well. Both of them, however, were empty. Remy sat beside her as she spoke.

"They were there when I got there. I think they knew I was coming in." She didn't bother looking at Remy as she spoke. "Two of them I managed to kill almost as soon as I realized I was in trouble. The others were just too many for me. I had to resort to other means to get away. Were you aware that they can slip under doorways by becoming a mist? I didn't have a clue."

"Yes. I'm sorry that I didn't tell you that. But I'm glad you managed to save yourself." She nodded and continued to watch the firefighters try to get some control over the fire. "I want you to come and live with us in the house. With me. I want you to come and live with me. I'm...I love you."

She turned to look at him and thought she could see something there. But she was much too smart to fall for that line. Turning back to the building, she watched it collapse in on itself and wondered if the bodies that were in there would ever be found.

"One of them spoke to me. He said to tell you that he's not going to let you win. He said that you owe him. Do you know what he means?" Skylar looked at Remy when he didn't answer. "Remy?"

"I don't. Honestly, I have no idea. I've killed a good many of them over the years that I couldn't even begin to count. If he feels I owe him something, I hope he comes to collect soon. I'm in the mood to kick some ass." Remy lifted her up and put her on his lap. She could feel his cock and wanted to pull away, but he held her. "I am hard, but that doesn't mean I want to have sex with you right now. I do, but it's not all I want from you."

"What then?" She leaned back against his chest and let him hold her. "I don't have anything at all to offer you. I can cook, but I don't care for it. I like having sex with you, but there's more to life than sex. And I suppose you need me to feed. By the way, I can eat regular food. I had an apple just before I left the building today."

"I can eat as well. I don't normally, but I can. Perhaps we can make a habit of it again. I should like to enjoy a meal with you." Skylar thought that was a good idea. "I don't care that you are homeless or penniless. Even if you had all the money in the world, it would matter little to me. What I do want from you, need from you is you to be with me. I enjoy having you by my side, and I even will admit that I enjoy arguing with you. You have a spark in your eyes that makes me crazy with lust."

"I've said this before, but you're very weird." He laughed, and she snuggled into his arms. "These creatures, no one else can see them but us, can they? Two of the officers were standing right next to one and neither of them noticed him. And I'm pretty sure that they converted one of them while I was waiting on you."

"They did. He stands there. See the look of confusion on his face?" Skylar saw him and nodded. "You will need to know more about them. And today I noticed some things that I had not before. Look at them, all of them. What do you see?"

Other than they were all faded out, nothing. Dark hair, the same sort of…she frowned. The exact same kind of dress. The tee-shirts were the same; the pants too. Then she looked at their faces. It was as if they were twins, or more. The closer she watched them, the more traits she could see that they had alike.

"Someone made them. They're clones." She could feel his head nodding. "The person who made them, do you know who it might be?"

"No. I have a feeling that the man in black knows." Skylar told him what his name was. "Hector? What a strange name. I suppose it is a fine name, but I have no idea why I thought it would be more magical."

"So did I." Skylar watched the newbie with new eyes. He was confused and none of the others, the malefactors, came to help him either. It was as if once he was made, he was on his own. She wondered how many of them made it after the first few months. "Do you think if I went over there and talked to him, he'd be able to tell me what he feels? I mean, he looks like someone took away all his mojo."

"Mojo?" Skylar shrugged. "I should like it if you didn't talk to him alone, but I can see that you are determined. Should you need me, all you need to do is look my way. I shall be there quickly."

Skylar walked across the street and stood next to the man. His uniform was gone now, and he was dressed as the others were. From faded shirt to boots. As he looked around, she caught his eye and thought of all the things she'd been able to unearth from Hector's mind.

"You're not supposed to be here." He looked at her, then away. "You can understand me. I know you can. Tell me what you're feeling right now."

"I don't know." He looked at her again. "I was doing my job, responding to a robbery when something moved over me. It...I think it bit me. I thought it was a bug, a big one, but now I'm not so sure. Do you know what happened to me?"

"You were converted to a killing machine. And there is nothing I can do to save you." He denied being a killing anything, but he did look at the others as they moved in and out of the crowd. "What do you feel?"

"That I have to die." Skylar felt badly about that. She'd been in a bad place a time or two and had thought about killing herself, but she wasn't sure that was going to help this creature. As she watched him, he began to take on characteristics of the others. The slow movement of his arms, his hair, once blond began to darken, and his face seemed to stretch and look gaunt. "What's happening to me? I feel…I need to kill you."

"And why do you have to kill me? What is it about me that makes you want to kill me?" He growled, and Skylar could see that he was fighting to keep control of his former self. "Tell me, officer. Why me?"

"All humans need to be extinguished. All of them." He reached for her then, his arm coming almost to her before the officer appeared again. He told her to run. "Now, get away now."

But she didn't. Instead when the creature took him, consumed him completely, Skylar reached her hand down into his gullet and touched his heart. This time, unlike the others, his was warm, not freezing cold. Wrapping her hand around it, she pulled it out and watched as the man crumbled to his knees. He looked at her, then mouthed the words "thank you" before he fell to the ground. Remy pulled her into his arms just as she dropped the heart.

"They're going to destroy us." Remy said something, but she couldn't understand it. "He had no idea what had happened to him. Not a clue that he was going to kill me. And when he died, he thanked me for finishing him off."

"Let's go to the house. We have to talk. There are things that I would like to know. Hector, you took his blood. I can feel the connection to him, but I believe there is more he is not telling us." Skylar nodded and moved with him to the car. The officer that she'd spoken to earlier was on his phone, but he only waved her on. She was leaving and if he wanted to talk to her, he'd have to find her. She'd had enough for one day.

"Hector is in a bad way. He has a sick wife and son." She tried to think what it was they had, but nothing was coming to her. It had been something that had come to her quickly when she'd been in his mind, and she was still, along with a great more information she'd gotten trying to sort it out. "They created these beings. His world did."

"What do you mean, created?" Remy looked at Davis when she didn't answer Davis. "She cannot mean that they brought them here to us to kill us? There is no way that they'd do that to us."

"I don't think they meant to. There were wars going on in their homeland, and they had made these beings to help fight it. They were ruthless and without thought. *Kill* was the only thing on their mind. And so they brought them here to help us. But something went wrong. I'm not sure what yet, but once they were left here, they began to convert every human that they came in contact with until they nearly overran the world. Now…I think now things are working up to that point again."

"They destroyed them before?" She nodded at Davis. "Then why don't they do it again? I mean, they should be able to if they made them, don't you think?"

"They are dying themselves." Skylar looked out the window. "Something is happening where they are. Their whole race is dying and they're afraid it has to do with the creatures that roam our earth. They're thinking that if they kill them all, or we do, they'll find a way to heal themselves."

"But you don't believe that." Skylar shook her head at Remy. "These beings, who created them? He would have used his own blood to have made them. And I would guess a part of their magic. And I'm thinking a great deal of magic if the way they created our home is any indication."

"They didn't create the building. I'm not entirely sure what happened there, but Hector is just as confused about it as we are. I think something else helped. I just can't figure out who." Skylar waited for what she'd said sink in. Remy looked at her for several seconds and when he finally got it, he began shaking his head.

"That means there are more than just Hector here, right? I mean, as you said there are more of them there in their realm but there are more here, on this earth. They think...they're more afraid now than they were before, aren't they? Of us, I mean."

"As they well should be." Skylar leaned back on the seat, weak now with all that she'd gone through. She had no idea what was in store for them now, especially her, but she had a feeling it was going to be a long time before she felt like she was normal. Looking at Davis and then Remy, she wondered if she should tell them the rest and decided that she was just too tired. Closing her eyes, she let sleep take her under.

Chapter 6

The call came out just as they were sitting down to dinner. Remy was afraid to let Skylar go, but in the end he was afraid to leave her alone too. So they moved out of the building and into the van that had come earlier today.

The malefactors had been sighted near a hospital. The new computers, with a very advanced system in it, had set off an alarm that had sounded throughout the house. Remy had been startled to see how much information that could be had from them would help. He decided that someone would need to be watching the computers, keeping an eye on movements rather than the alarm telling them that there were more than a dozen gathered in one place.

"They're going in. We have to stop them." He knew that, but the problem was, how? Not without others seeing them do it. "I have an idea. We can only see them, right? I mean, even their body once they are dead?"

"Yes, so far as I know, only we can see them. Perhaps a few humans can see them that have had some magic in their lives, but not many of those are willing to help us."

Remy didn't want to think about being covered in blood again, but there was nothing for it. The computer told them that there were well over a hundred of the creatures there.

"Then why can't we do the same? Become invisible, I mean. And if we just stab our hands into their chest instead of down their throats, I think things would go much faster too." Davis had a point. They would look stupid fighting something that wasn't there that they could see. "How long has it been since you tried it that way?"

"Never." He shifted on the seat when Davis looked at him hard. "My hand was down this throat, and I touched his heart. It worked. I never thought to try anything differently. What did you do to kill them?"

"I've never done it before the other day with you. Remember? I'm a newbie too. That guy, Hector, just changed me over. And I know that Skylar here has done it the way you showed her. Why don't we give my way a shot? If it doesn't work, then what are we out? Nothing. As for the cloaking thing? I think we can just...I have no idea, but what if we just think about not being seen?" Remy closed his eyes and thought about shifting to a shadow. When Davis and Skylar laughed, he looked at them. "It worked. I mean I can see you because of what we are, but you're faded out. Not without color like they are but sort of shadowy. And if this heart thing doesn't work, then we go back to your way. No one will ever know the difference. And it might just work."

"It might." He thought, however, that it would work and that frightened him just a little. Remy knew that his strength had grown since he and Skylar had gotten together. And when they touched their marks, it was as if an explosion went off. Everything around them vibrated or seemed to move. He wondered if they were to focus all that power outward, what it would do to the malefactors.

As soon as the van stopped in front of the hospital, Remy knew they were going to have their work cut out for them. There had to be more than the computer had said. They were thick in the entrance. As soon as he was close enough to one of the creatures, the thing turned on him and sliced his hand toward his face. It took him a moment to realize that the thing had a sword. Some of them even had long blades and knives. Remy had just missed having his head removed. They were armed now, it seemed.

He nearly reached into the thing's throat, but saw Skylar smash her hand, and that was just what it looked like she'd done, into the malefactor's chest and pull his beating heart out. As the thing fell, his heart landing on his dead body, she moved to the next one. Remy decided that as soon as they got home, he was fucking her as hard as she'd let him. Christ, she was something else.

They killed ten before they were in the door. The bodies were piling up, but no one but them noticed it. Even the revolving door took no notice of the bodies as it rolled around and round, cutting the bodies in half as it went. The first cubical he came to, Remy knew why they were here.

There were injured and dying humans everywhere. Three and four of them, one per gurney in each room. The staff running around trying to save as many as they could and the malefactors converting those that were ignored. He came upon one of them leaning into a young boy when Remy tossed him back.

"You." Remy waited, hoping for something from the creature rather than the spittle that came from his mouth.

"Master wishes to see you. He has a deal. He wants to deal with you."

"No." Before the thing could speak again, Remy pulled his heart out and was struck by the difference almost immediately. This one's heart was blue, as blue as the oceans. And it looked bigger, healthier than the other ones. But this creature wasn't a recruit, nor was he a second generation. He was one of the originals, he thought.

Remy had no time to stop and think. But he did pull a bag off the table near where he was and put the heart in it. He wasn't sure what good it would do, but he thought maybe he could compare it to another one. One of the other dead that he dealt with.

It took them nearly two hours of going door to door in the big hospital. They were only stopped twice by one or more saying the master wanted to talk to them. And even then it hadn't slowed them any. Davis told him when he asked him if he'd seen Skylar, but he said that she'd gone down when they'd gone up. He headed that way, looking in the doors as he went just in case. By the time he was in the sublevels, Remy had killed two more of the blue-hearted recruits. He heard her before he saw her.

"What do you mean you have a message for me? I don't know you. What sort of message could you have for me?" The thing laughed and Remy paused. He could see Skylar, at least her back. But the creature he could see clearly through the small seam where the door was attached to the frame. "Let go of the kid and I'll talk to you."

He was holding a child as a shield. The kid looked to be already dead. His head had been injured badly in whatever had brought the lot of people into the hospital.

He thought it has been an accident but wasn't entirely sure.

"My master wishes to deal with you. He said that he can offer you everything that you wish." Remy smiled when Skylar snorted. "You can have so much should you only talk to him."

"Talking to you is enough, thanks. You're giving me a migraine." The thing snarled at her, and he wondered if he knew how lucky he was that she'd found the thing and not him. He would have been dead by now. "What kind of master do you have? Stupid comes to mind. And so does-"

"He is master of all. You too soon enough." He heard Skylar snort again and had to cover his mouth to laugh. "You scoff him? You dare defy him? He is a man with vision. A man to reckon with."

"Yeah, yeah. He's the almighty Oz. Whatever. What I want from you is to tell me why you're not like the others. Why do you never shut up, first of all? The others can't talk." The being said something, and Remy leaned in closer to hear him. "I really don't care what your master is or what he thinks he is. I asked you a fucking question. Answer me."

The compulsion was there. Strong and demanding. The creature, he could see, was fighting it, but it was a losing battle. Remy stepped around the doorway just as the thing started talking.

"I have been given a special boon. A bit of his blood as well as magic from him. He had to put it into me. The first of my kind and now there will be many." Remy moved up behind Skylar, and she didn't look at him, but she knew he was there. "The mighty master has given some of us his blood and we are powerful beyond compare. We can talk to him, tell him of our plans, and he listens. We will conquer this world as we will all the others."

"He certainly does have grandiose plans, your master. I don't suppose he told you how he was going to carry this out. I mean, having you talk might be a way for a few people to kill themselves, but I doubt that it would be enough to take over the entire world." Skylar looked at him as she continued. "Do you think this fuck knows anything? I doubt it. Giving him the ability to talk aside, I bet he doesn't know shit."

Before he could comment, the monster took a step toward them. "I know everything. He is going to kill all the humans that will not convert. And those men and women will be such an army that no one, not even you with your puny powers, will be able to defeat us."

"Powers?" Skylar looked at him, then back at the creature. "What are you talking about? What powers do you think I have?"

The creature looked at him, then at Skylar. His smile was full of teeth. His face had a look of one who thought he knew the answer to the biggest joke of all. When he took a second step toward them, Skylar put up her hand at the same time he did. Their marks touched, and the creature fell back.

As he lay there staring up at them with dead, vacant eyes, Skylar turned to him. She looked…he thought afraid, but that soon turned to being pissed off. Remy took a step back, then another when she advanced on him.

"You killed him." Remy shook his head. "You did. I had it under control, and I was getting information. Why did you blast him? We could have gotten so much more."

"We did it." She shook her head. "We did it, Skylar. When we touched. Remember? The power that comes when we do that? We took him out. Together."

She stared at the marks on her arm, then at his. He could see her mind working, but he wasn't sure if that was a good thing or not. When she looked up at him, he knew for a moment that he was going to die. Then she smiled.

"We can kill them this way." He nodded, not sure where she might be going with this. "Together we have the makings of a bomb. Or a ray gun. Something. But we can kill them without getting close. And I'm betting we can take out a lot of them at once too."

"A weapon." She nodded. Remy had never been one to use a weapon. The marks on his hips made him crazy enough. He realized then that he'd never asked her about hers. Now was as good a time as any, he supposed. "Those guns on our legs, do you know what they're meant for?"

She nodded slowly. Whatever she knew, he wasn't at all sure he wanted her to tell him. When she put her hand over her own hip, he had a feeling she was going to show him. Before he could tell her no, a weapon appeared in her hand.

"We need only to think about having it in our hands." He nodded, pulling his hands as far from his hips as he could. "I read it in Hector's mind. Same with the wings. I've not tried them as yet, but I know that we can use them. We'll be able to go great distances without much of a time lapse."

"They're too small to lift us." She shook her head, and he nodded. "Yes. They are. I've seen them. And in order for them to be enough to lift us, they'd be much bigger."

"Think of them, Remy. Think of your wings." He tried his best to think of anything other than the wings on his back. But, of course, it was all he could think of. The burn was the first thing he felt.

Remy didn't feel pain, just the little burn, but it was gone in seconds. He thought maybe it had been nothing, but then he looked at Skylar's face. She looked so shocked that he turned to see what was behind him. That was when he saw them, or at least one of them.

They were dark, a black so dark it seemed to glow with it, and huge. Stretching from over his head to the floor, they seemed much bigger than he'd ever need. But when she moaned, he knew that for whatever reason, she was shifting as well. Her wings were a match to his in color and fullness but just a little smaller.

"Remy, what the fuck are we?" He had no idea and told her that. Before this he'd thought of himself as just a warrior. This...these things changed everything. "I want to go home."

"All right, love." He had a burst of a thought and said it before he could think. "Shall we fly?"

Her fist to his belly didn't hurt, but he did groan. She was strong. Stronger than she'd been when he'd first met her. And now with the wings and the weapons, Remy was a little afraid of whatever else might happen to them.

~~~

Their wings fit against their bodies with just a thought. Skylar wanted to run out of the building they were in and try them out. But she had a feeling that they needed to keep them secret for a while. She had seen in Hector's mind that they would have powers and that they only needed to will them to use them, but he didn't seem to know what they might have. Christ, she had wings.

"Got a few of them cornered up on the roof top. I saw a couple of them jump. They don't bounce well, just in case you were wondering." Davis looked at Remy, then her. "Something is different about you two. You feed yet?"

"Not yet." Remy reached for her hand. "We might have a way to take care of a lot of them at once. I'd like to try it out. I don't know if it will work or not, but we'll see."

As they made their way to the upper floors, Skylar noticed that no one seemed to take any notice of them still. She was glad for that because she had blood all over her shirt and pants. Remy was covered in what looked like blue blood, and she wondered then if he'd had an encounter with one of the creatures in the basement, but it was Davis that had her attention. The man was not just covered in blood, but he looked as if he'd bathed in it. She asked him what had happened.

"I have a sword." He put his hand on his hip. As suddenly as it filled his hand, Davis seemed to grow larger in size. "I don't know what made me think of that new brand I have on me, but there it was. I can swing it like nobody's business too."

Skylar started to ask him if he had wings as well, but Remy shook his head. Why? she wondered. Then she remembered that they were marked differently. Skylar wondered if there was something special about them, then remembered Hector's thoughts. They were the elite warriors. Elite warriors of what, she didn't have a clue, but nodded as they made their way to the elevator. As soon as they made it through the barricade that Davis had set up, she knew a real kind of fear.

There were perhaps fifty of the creatures. They were huddled in the corner of the roof and looked as if they had not a single fear about what was happening. Skylar saw the blue creature when two of the front ones shifted on their feet. Skylar walked to the crowd and pulled him forward. But it was Remy that did the talking this time.

"I've a need to speak to you." The thing snarled at him, and she kicked out knocking him down so that he fell to his knees. Two of the others came forward and she simply killed one of them. That backed them all up. "Now that we've established who is in charge, we can—"

"You think that you rule here?" The blue man laughed. "You will be dead soon enough, and we will rule. The master has said as much to us. He will be the grand master of this entire realm."

"Yeah, we've heard that shit before." She looked at Remy before continuing. "I suppose he's made you something else. Given you something special that makes you think we can't kill you."

"He has. I am all powerful." To prove his point, he turned to the man behind him and snapped his fingers. The being dropped to the floor in an instant. "See? And I shall do the same to you when I am ready."

"And this power? You got it from his blood." The thing looked shocked, then recovered quickly when Remy laughed at him. "We know more than you think we do. Like, for instance, we know that you aren't as all powerful as you think you are. I, myself, just killed one of your kind. Then there is the added fact that we have you where we want you. This way when you're all killed, we can simply dump your remains over the top here and be done with you."

"You lie." Remy put his arms over his chest and looked very impressive. Skylar had to bring her thoughts to a halt because all she could think about was having him naked while he did that. She focused as much attention on the creature as she could. "Master said that we would be the superior race. That once all you humans are gone, we'll take over other worlds and rule there as well. He has said to me personally that I would be in charge of a single kingdom."

"Good for you. But you're not going to live long enough to do anything of the kind." Remy knelt down to his level and put his hand to his chest. There was pain on the creature's face, but he didn't cry out. "I'm going to take your heart out and drink from it as you lay watching me."

"No." The being tried to pull away, but Remy had him. "Please. You cannot kill me. I am a chosen one."

"Chosen to do what?" The being bit his lips hard not to answer Remy. Blood, blue and glossy, dripped from the wound he was making with his fangs. "What were you chosen to do?"

"I am to make as many of me as I can. I am to kill you, the renegade, and bring your hearts to the master. He will feast on you, serve you up for all of us to enjoy and bask in your deaths." Remy looked at her and then at the creature again, asking him what he was called. "Adherent. I am his servant. The others we call soldiers."

"Adherent? Doesn't that mean follower or something like that? Doesn't sound to me like you're in charge but someone that simply does what he's told." Remy grinned at her as she continued. "I'd call them lapdogs or maybe peons. That'll make you nothing in the long line of fools."

"Not a fool. I am going to rule." But Skylar could see that he was skeptical. He looked around at the others before speaking again. "What will you do with them? The master will be most displeased if you harm them. I shall tell him that you did what you must."

"You're going to be right about that, but you won't be telling him." Remy stood up and pulled her to him. "You are going to be our test. We want to see if our puny powers, as you call them, are enough to destroy the lot of you."

"You wish to kill me?" He sounded so incredulous that Skylar laughed. "I am not like the soldiers. I am superior."

Her arm slid along Remy's, and she felt the power. As soon as their marks touched, she knew that they were stronger than ever before. She nodded at Davis to come to them. Once he touched her arm to his, the power took her breath away.

She was glad that Remy had been the one directing the blast. She might have missed and hit one of them. Skylar was trembling with energy. And when the blast hit the soldiers and the adherent, she felt as if she'd been drained. The creatures not only died but they degenerated into nothingness in seconds.

"Christ." Davis couldn't have expressed it any better and was glad that he'd said it. As they parted, each of them dropped to the ground and sat there. The place where the creatures had been wasn't even scorched. There wasn't anything to ever show that they'd been there but a small stone. Skylar leaned over and picked it up.

"It's an agate." She handed it to Remy and leaned back on her hands. "The blue guy, the adherent, he said that he was given something to make him special. Could that be it? Or was it here before."

Remy passed it to Davis, who held it over his head. "Nah, it was his. See the blue vein in it. I'd bet anything this is what you get when you kill one of them blue guys."

Remy stood up when she did. They both went to the lower floors, and Davis was right behind them. The first floor they stopped on was the fifth. It took them several minutes of looking, and just when they were ready to give up, Davis found another agate. Then they went to the basement.

There were others there, humans, and each of them turned to them when the elevator door opened up. The first one turned back to picking up the broken table while the other two stared. Skylar had a moment of worry until they too turned back to the job. She picked up a large hunk of wood and tossed it into the trash bin, and there it lay. She picked the agate up.

This one was larger than the other two. When she asked to see them, both Remy and Davis held it out. As soon as hers was close, they lit up. Remy closed his hand over his.

"We should do this at home." Davis nodded, and she thought he was right. "That way if it brings the big master guy, we'll be able to control things better. I'm just hoping it will get past the protection."

Chapter 7

Remy put the three stones in small containers he'd found. He marked them with the date as well as where they'd gotten them. Then he put the heart he'd gotten in the freezer. He had no idea what to do with it and thought that saving it for someone who knew would help. Maybe the person could find out what he couldn't even guess. Davis was at the computer making a file for all the information that they'd gotten that day. Skylar was helping him. Something about the stones bothered him, and Remy just couldn't put his finger on it.

"I was looking up some information on agates. There is a great deal about them that I didn't know." She grinned at him. "I've been looking up the mythical powers that might be associated with them. I don't know which agate this is, so I was just trying to find some images. Would you like to help me?"

Remy sat beside her and decided that his need to touch her was more than he could let go. Picking her up, he put her on his lap and held her there. She only made him harder when she squirmed around a little to get comfortable. Christ, he wanted her again. Clearing his throat, he tried to think why he was sitting here and not fucking her in his bedroom.

"These are different colors. Do you know why? I mean, one is white with some kind of wiggly lines in it and the other two are darker, more reds in them." She pulled up a picture on the computer, and they scrolled through the images when Davis stopped her. "That one. See how the colors seem to blend together into some sort of cohesive line?"

"It says it's a fire agate. And that it is often used in spells to increase communication in writing and speaking. Well, that sort of explains why they would have it. You said that none of the others could speak." Remy nodded, but he was reading on to the other properties of the stone.

"The white one we have, it looks like a lacy agate. They are said to be particularly useful for protection. Like a webbing around the person. Do you suppose that he gave that adherent one to keep him safe from us?" Davis laughed as Skylar continued. "I know it didn't, but do you think he thought it would?"

"I'd say this master, or whatever he is, he's going to keep making them guys until we can shut him down. We caught three of them today. How many others do you suppose are out there? And you think he's making more of himself?" Remy wasn't sure who was making them, but he thought that Davis was right. When Davis stood up and stretched, he looked at them. "I'm going up to my rooms. Damned nice ones too, just so you know. And that kitchen is stocked with everything a man like me would ever want."

After he left, Skylar leaned back on his chest. He loved holding her like this. There was something so soft about her right now that he wanted to keep her here forever. When she stood up, he watched her as she made her way around the room.

"I've not seen much of the house, but this room and the one we came in to get here. Have you?" Shaking his head, he stood up too. "I want to explore. And I'm hungry. I could eat a horse."

He followed, but he had to adjust his cock twice before he was able to speak. Christ, this woman could do to him what no other had done. Make him feel like an angry bull.

They entered a large room that he thought was a living room. There were several large overstuffed chairs around as well as three large couches that faced a fireplace as big as his first home.

He tried hard to remember the face of his wife and children and started to pull open the locket around his neck that had been his wife's. But he didn't. He did pull it to his mouth and kissed it, then slipped it into his shirt. Another time, he thought, just not right now.

After the living room, they entered the two rooms on this level. There was what he could only call a reading room. Library seemed so...well, it didn't suit as well. There were five walls in this room, all of them covered in floor-to-ceiling shelves brimming with books. A huge gas fireplace sat against one of the walls, and there were windows on either side of it. The large overstuffed chairs seemed to be begging to be used, and he sat in one of the leather ones and felt the buttery softness of it before looking up at Skylar.

"This is lovely. I could stand to sit here for hours on end just to enjoy the smell of it." She sat in one of the other chairs and pulled a beautiful afghan over her legs. "You look well there. Like you belong."

"I've always dreamed of a room like this. So full of books that you'd never get through them all." She looked around, then frowned. "Actually, this is exactly what I had in mind. Including the five walls. Do you suppose Hector read my mind?"

He had no idea, but he looked around the room. There were touches that he'd thought of too. Like the gas fireplace. When he'd been married, it had been a chore to keep the house even warm, much less hot. Frowning himself, he thought of the fireplace he'd wanted in the bedroom.

"We need to go and see our room." He stood up so quickly that he knocked the chair back. It didn't fall, but it was still vibrating when he pulled Skylar from the chair. As they headed up the staircase, he took note of the rest of the house. The dining room with the floor-to-ceiling windows there as well. The long table that could seat at least two dozen people. The hallway blurred by them, the planters full of greenery swayed as he practically ran past them. But as soon as he entered, Remy came to a complete stop.

"It's my dream of a room." He moved in slowly, almost reverently. "My wife, so long ago, we had nothing much to speak of. A home, children, but little else. I was a warrior then, working hard to make them a better life. But when I was alone, sitting in some camp awaiting orders, I would think of the room I'd like for her. This was it."

"It's beautiful." He didn't bother looking at Skylar as he went to the bed. "I didn't know you were married. You never mentioned her before."

"It was long ago. Many…eighteen hundred years or so." Remy heard the short intake of her breath, but didn't think about it. "I forget her face. And those of my children. I miss them so much at times."

The bed was a large four poster one. The solid oak posts were plain, but they had grain to them that had him running his hand over it. The smoothness of the wood made him think it was old, the wood's satiny feel from many hands touching it.

The furniture was made of the same solid wood. No cutting work done to mar the lovely surface but a grain that nearly popped in its brilliance. There were knobs on the drawers that made him reach out to wrap his hand around them. Remy smiled when they filled his hand like Skylar's warm breast did. Turning to speak to her, he noticed that he was alone.

He started after her, nearly did go when he spied the framed picture. It was an old one, the frame nearly as old as he was. Picking it up with shaking fingers, he held it to the light to see the images there. They were his family. All of them.

His son had been ten; his twin daughters were nearly seven when they were killed. His wife had been in her twenty-third year and fat with their child. The men who had come, men no less horrible than the malefactors he dealt with now. They had killed them. Killed them because they felt as if Remy had fought for the wrong cause.

The picture was the one in the locket he wore. It was a grainy picture. One that was more dark than light. He smiled at the look in his son's face, the look that told him he'd rather be playing than sitting for such a thing. His daughters were as beautiful as their mother. Setting it down again, Remy took off the locket and hung it over the frame. He had moved on finally and was more than ready to begin his life.

Not that he'd ever forget them. Never that but he did need to make a life now and he had Skylar to thank for that. As he made his way down the hall again, this time at a more sedate pace, he smiled when he thought of what he was going to do to his woman as soon as he found her. Hopefully she'd be alone.

~~~

Skylar punched the bag again and felt the bones in her fingers protest. The fucker was married. He'd never told her that. She jammed her fist into the bag again and again imagining it to be his body, his head she was hitting. When the bag was suddenly gone, her fist went wide and she fell on her ass. The man of her misery was standing over her laughing.

"Get out." He took a step back from her and that for whatever reason pissed her off. Standing up she moved around him to use the weights. She was going to burn this anger off even if she had to be here for a week.

"What's the matter?" He was in her face again and she just managed not to hit him. "I thought we were going to test out the new bed."

"Your wife's bed." He looked confused, so she explained it to the asshole. "You said you were married. That the bedroom was what you wanted with her. You were going to fuck me in your wife's bedroom."

"My wife is dead." The words spoken so softly did nothing to cool her temper. But now it was directed at her, not him. "She died many years ago, as did my three children and the one she carried. Did you think I would do what we've done had I been married to her still?"

"I don't have a clue. But you didn't tell me." She tried her best to pull her temper in but it wasn't working. "You loved her. You love her still."

"I do." He moved to touch her, and she backed away. "Skylar, what is this about? I don't have a wife any longer. I have missed her a great deal, but you have brought me such joy."

"You mean someone you can fuck readily?" She closed her mouth when she saw that she'd hurt him. He started to walk away, then turned abruptly and grabbed her.

"You think that this is all I feel for you?" He slammed her against the wall, his body pressing against hers so hard it was as if he were trying to become a part of her. "I will show you what I want from you."

Her clothes were suddenly gone. Not torn away but simply gone. When she wrapped her hands over his shoulders to hold him to her, she felt hot, raw skin. His muscles were bunched under her fingers, and she felt his cock at her entrance.

Remy slammed into her. Her body, already highly charged came apart with his first thrust. His mouth didn't so much take her as he ate at her, biting deeply into her shoulder and throat. Blood poured from the wounds as he continued taking her hard and fast, his bites making it harder and harder for her to think of anything but what he was doing to her.

"Come again. Now." Her body did as he commanded and even spiked up to come again when she was still reeling from the second one. His body shook the wall behind her, and his fingers dug deeply into her hips as he pounded her hard. When he sank his teeth into her throat again, Skylar screamed out her release, her body coming apart twice before she felt him seal the wounds at her throat.

But he wasn't finished with her. Pulling his body from hers, he turned her around, bent her over the work bench beside them, and entered her pussy. His hands were bruising her, leaving a mark that she would cherish for as long as it was there. Still, he fucked her, moving the equipment across the room a foot with each hard fuck.

His hand coming down across her ass startled her. She turned to look at him when he hit her again and again. While it was painful to a degree, she felt as if he were bringing her closer to an epic climax that was going to take her breath away. And when he reached between her legs, bending nearly in half to touch her, Skylar screamed out her climax even as he bit deeply into her shoulder.

The room blurred as she felt his cum fill her. She came again when he released, his hot juices bringing her over and over until she was weak with it. Skylar was holding onto her consciousness with all she had, and she had a feeling he wasn't finished with her yet. But when he picked her up in his arms like a babe and held her, she wrapped her arms around him and held him to her. His voice when he spoke finally was low, harsh but nearly a whisper.

"She was burned with my children. After they raped her. All of them having their turns with her, they set the house aflame and then the barn, still filled with the few animals we had." Skylar lay very still as he continued. "She must have hid the children. There was a root cellar beneath the kitchen that she used, and that was where I found them. Burned huddled together as they did when they slept."

He stood up, taking her with him. He still held her tenderly and held her in his arms as he made his way up the stairs to the bedroom. He never spoke as he walked, and Skylar let the tears fall for what she'd done to him. When he laid her on the bed, his naked body before her, she sat up and ran her fingers over the scar that was on his chest.

"What happened here?" He put his hand over hers and then took hers to his mouth. After kissing it, he placed it over his heart and stared at her before speaking.

"The day that Hector found me there was a great battle. I had hoped...I had planned to die that day. End my life as surely as my wife and children had been killed. But he only touched me. The pike that was here, coming from the back to the front seemed to be nothing any longer as it was pulled from me." He ran his hand down to the scar, then took her hand in his again. "I wished for death more than once in all these years. I have been alive...nay, nearly dead in my heart, but walking for over eighteen hundred years. I didn't live again until you came into my life."

"I love you." He pulled her into his arms, holding her as softly as he did firmly. "I'm so sorry for what I said to you. I had no right to—"

The fingers over her mouth silenced her. "There is no reason for you to be sorry. You had no way of knowing my past any more than I do yours. For all I know, you can have several husbands in your life. But I care not to hear about them. I am in love with you. And will be for the rest of our days."

"I have no husband. No boyfriend either. Not even much of a life." She sat on the bed when he let her go. And when he went to the other side of the bed, she crawled under the covers with him. "My father was a great man. A little forgetful but a wonderful loving father. My mom died when I was born, so he was both of them for me. And when he died…when he died it was all I could do to survive. But the bills…there were so many of them that at first I just paid what I could. Then I realized that they weren't all his."

"What happened?" Skylar was almost afraid to tell him. A man who had given up so much just so that his wife could have a better way of life. "Tell me."

"There was a house keeper. She came in twice a week to clean for him and me. Dad didn't care if the house looked like a bomb went off in it so long as he could come home from work and play in his shop. I worked a lot, so it was nice to have someone come in and dust and sweep for us. But she was robbing us. She took his credit cards and mine and bought hundreds of thousands of dollars of things I will never see. Every time the card was maxed out, she'd take another one, or worse yet, apply for more. Dad had over thirty credit cards in his name when he died, and he had actually only applied for two. I had two as well, but when it was over, they found over twenty in my name. And there was little to nothing we could do about it."

"Nothing? Why not? There are laws about such things. I have seen them." She loved the way he got all protective of her and smiled at him. "You have a very sappy look in your face right now."

"Thanks." After slapping him on the chest, she laid her head on it. "Dad had signed the applications. I had no way to dispute them so I was named on the cards as well. Not my signature, but I was still responsible for them as his heir. We…I lost it all. My parents' home, the car, and my education. Plus every job I have, the creditors take a large chunk of it to pay it all. So that leaves me little to nothing to eat and live off of."

"You shall pay them off with my money." She sat up and looked down at him. "Would you like to pay them off with our money?"

"Nice save." She lay back down. "I will think about it. It's a lot of money. I mean a lot. Dad had great credit as did I and now it's all shit."

"I have a great deal of money that I have no use for. I have no need for food, just you. I have a house now, thanks to you. And a good job, that I get to work with you in. I have more than a man should."

"You're a sap." He laughed and rolled her to her back. "I love you, Rembrandt. Do you have a last name?"

"I do, it is Rembrandt. My first name…I have not used it in more years than I can remember. I don't even remember it now." Skylar had a feeling he knew it but for some reason it was too painful for him. "I like that you call me Remy. Especially when you scream it out at the top of your lungs when you reach your peak."

"You make me scream all kinds of things when I come." His kiss, gentle and full of love, took her breath away. "I truly am sorry for what I said to you."

"Don't worry on it. I have…it's forgotten." He frowned at her. "The stones are not left behind. They are a part of the men."

Her mind was still catching up to his when he leapt from the bed. She was looking for clothing when she realized that he was dressed and leaving her. Putting her fingers in her mouth and blowing, she watched as he came to a startled stop.

"Clothing. How do you do that?" He told her to think about them. "Yeah, that's not what I meant. I mean how do I —?" She wasn't just dressed but in the sloppy clothes she preferred.

"I have done this for years. Most helpful when you need to take off in a hurry." When she asked him what would have him naked and leaving somewhere in a hurry, he came back and kissed her nose. "I have not been a celibate man, my dear. Women adore me."

"Those women are nuts. You are neither charming nor adorable." He swatted her bottom and moved to the door. "And you're an asshole."

"Perhaps. But I am your asshole and you love me." He was whistling when he left the room this time, and she started to follow. Stomping her way into the kitchen to get a sandwich, she was met by a woman dressed all in black. And she looked like she could take her on and come out on top, despite all her newly found powers.

"You'd be the missus of the house?" Skylar nodded. "I'm Ann Hathaway, no relation to the star. She's beautiful and I can cook."

If it was a joke, Skylar didn't get it. "Hum, how did you get here? And who hired you to…what are you here for?"

"Cook. And clean. Though I think this place will need more than me. The man, Hector, said that you would need me to hire help as you needed it. Right?" She nodded. "I have a granddaughter, she's a good girl. Having a baby soon out of the wedlock, but nowadays that's not so bad."

"No. I suppose not." Skylar sat when she told her to and stared at the food that was set in front of her. "You know this might work better if I knew…what are you?"

"Cook and a bit more." She sat down across from her. "I'm a telepath. My granddaughter too, and so will the baby, I would imagine. Hector told me we'd be safe here. That true?"

"Yes. You're here with some very powerful beings." She nodded and stood up. "I don't understand why he thinks we'll need a cook. I mean, someone to clean, yes, but a cook? We're not…"

"He said you eat. But the other man, Rembrandt, he's a vampire warrior." Again she nodded and felt foolish for it and said yes. "That Mr. Brown, he eats food too. But said he had to bite too. I'm not food for any of you. Nor will be my family."

"No, there will be no biting of the help." She nodded and put a large glass of tea in front of her plate. "So…will you live here too? I would prefer that did if you don't mind. I think you're going to be safer here. And I guess we'll need a medical staff too."

"They arrived an hour ago. Setting up the clinic now. It's in the sublevels, did you know that?" She didn't but nodded. "Those men, there are ten of them. Some of them are working in the clinic. Others are in the command room, they called it. The one with all the computers. They said that this house was safe in more ways than just you guys being here."

Skylar nodded. "Do you need to be protected? I mean more than with just some muscle? You don't have to tell me, but it might help us keep you safe."

Ann got up and started wiping down the already spotless counter. Skylar knew that there was food in all the cabinets and that the pantry was full as well. When they returned from the hospital, there had been several trucks at the back of the house and someone had started to unload them. She now assumed it was Ann.

"There's this ex-husband of mine. He's...well, he's got it in his head that I should be still his wife. We quit him a few years ago while he was in prison for murder. I don't want him coming around here." Skylar didn't either but let Ann continue. "He thinks because we have this power...he thinks I can give him the horse races. Or some crap like that. And he's hoping that this baby of my little girl's is a boy. He wants to raise him up in his image."

Skylar laughed, and Ann smiled. "I think we can keep him away. And all the more reason for you to live here with us. If you want something more, like your own place, we can accommodate you in that department as well."

"No. I like my rooms just fine. They're on back there with my granddaughter's. And somebody went and gave her all the bedding and stuff she's gonna need for the little one." Ann flushed. "That doctor downstairs, Doctor Weston Page, already gave her an examination and said she was fit. Good to know since we didn't have any insurance from before this and I don't trust them clinic doctors much."

After Skylar made sure Ann had everything she needed, she decided to go to the upper levels again. This time she was determined to look around. But when she entered the first room, she stood there for several seconds, realizing what was happening in the house. Backing out of the completed room, she made her way to find Remy. She wanted to talk about what she thought was happening over with him before she freaked out.

Chapter 8

Master walked around the large building. He needed to go to ground soon. After dealing with the massacre at the hospital, he needed to rest. But he wanted to do something so completely not work related that he found just walking out in the twilight was helping. The noise behind him had him closing his eyes in frustration.

"Master?" He turned slowly and looked at the man who had come out to join him uninvited. "I have been all over the area five times and sent in the best soldiers we have and there is no trace of the elements."

He knew it. They had taken them. Or the janitorial service had swept them up when they made their rounds not having a clue what they'd done. Nodding once, he walked away from the adherent he'd only made this morning. But apparently he wasn't finished.

"What is it?" The man backed up, and he had to take in a long slow breath and let it out just as slowly. "I lost over fifty men today, three of them my seconds. What could you possibly tell me now that will make my day worse?"

"Five more of the soldiers have taken their own lives." Master started cursing. It was a habit he'd only just picked up recently and he thought he was pretty good at it. When he finished, he looked at the adherent and growled low when he opened his mouth.

"Go away." The man opened his mouth again, but Master cut him off. "If you speak, even to tell me goodbye, I will kill you myself. And I can assure you it will not be as easy a death as my men suffered on the top of that building."

He turned and left. Master walked again. This time he knew that no matter if he walked five thousand times around the building, it would no longer calm him. Someone was going to have to pay for today.

Opening his mouth wide, he let his teeth, rows and rows of sharp fangs, slide into place. His tongue slashed out of his mouth and cut a gash into his arm. Master then brought the wound to his mouth and suckled hard at it but not enough to fill him. That would never do. Instead he looked to the sky and took to it, his wings, black as soot and full as the oceans filled out, and he soared higher.

His body, a darker hue than his wings, blocked out the stars as he moved in the night. Flapping his enormous wings, he felt his body shift and take the form of what he truly was. A monster. A huge blood sucking, flesh eating monster. And Master loved this self.

Claws replaced his hands, his head elongated until his chin nearly touched his chest in a long point at each end. Scales appeared on his back and body, his feet were clawed as well, but his feet webbed to help him in flight. Master let his body change more, taking on his appearance that he'd been given when he'd gotten here. His ears stretched. His hearing became more acute. As his eyes turned to a dark blood red, he felt them change as well. He knew that he could see as far as he'd ever want or need.

The men in the park below him seemed to call to him. Master lowered his body down to the earth to see how many there were and if he could take them all at once. He didn't need them all to fill his need, but the more humans to die now by his hand was less that he'd have to deal with later. Plus there was the added bonus that he'd get to change one or two of them. The five men were huddled together around a basketball court. Master landed not far from them. And as much as he hated to do so, after feeling so good for a time, he shifted his body back to his earthly form and waited on the pain of his bones moving before walking.

Easy pickings, he called this type of feeding. He'd go in, take two by the throat, and feed from the strongest one. The other three he would hold in thrall until he finished his meal, then kill them as well. Changing them would have to come after he had his fill.

"Stay." When the first one saw him, he reached for something in his pocket. While a gun would not kill him, stupid humans, it would put a damper on his fun. When the men obeyed his command, he pulled the first one to him and tore out his throat. No longer caring to feed first, he killed the next man as well. Their pitiful bodies lay there bleeding out while he captured the site of the next man.

"Fuck me." The man began to take of his pants, and Master watched. He wasn't going to let him touch him with his dick, but to watch him do as he was told amused him. Master waited while he took his shirt and pants off and stood before him, naked. "I've changed my mind. I want you to suck off that man while I feed from you."

The second man opened his pants, and his cock slid out. It was thick and hard, but it still did nothing for Master. Long ago he'd lost all ability to get any interest in sex at all. He just liked watching the control he had over others by using it against them.

The first man dropped to his knees and took the other man into his mouth. Master watched uninterested but did walk up to the third man. He jerked his head back and sank his fangs, all of them, into his throat, tearing it out while he drank greedily from him. As he died, his body simply giving up, Master dropped him on the ground and stepped to the man getting his cock blown.

He had a scent about him. It wasn't until he was ready to sink his fangs into him that he realized he wasn't human. Backing from him, the man looked at him as he pulled his cock from the other man's mouth and kicked him away. This was going to be painful, and there was little Master could do about it now. Not in his current form.

The hard punch to his face made him feel like the man had used more than his fist to hit him. The second blow, this one to his stomach, had him falling to his knees. He was flying backward when he realized he should get the fuck out of there. But the big man, a wolf, shifted and tore into his leg as he started to leave the ground. Turning as he kicked backward, Master could see the bone and blood of his body as he used some of his power to throw the wolf back. But the damage to him was already done.

He would heal. Knowing that didn't make it any less painful. But he wouldn't die. His blood, his species, would see to that. But it would hurt. As he came back to the ground several yards away, his wings making the trees around the park sway and move, he blasted his magic at the wolf as he ran for cover. Master was still laughing when he got back to the building they were staying in. The wolf, he knew, was as dead as the other men.

There was no one around when he got to his room. It was, as it should have been, the biggest one in the building. They had moved into it only a few days ago, and he had been adjusting it to suit his needs. It was hard work doing this and nearly drained him each day that he did only a little of what he wanted. So far there was only him and five adherents staying there. All the soldiers were out converting as many humans as they could. Or they had better be.

He was going to have an army that would simply take over the world, Master thought as he tended his wound. This world, as well as any others he could find, were going to be his as soon as he got his plan perfect here. It was getting there, just not as quickly as he'd hoped. Right now, at this moment, he was just gathering his fold. A trick he'd learned on his home planet, the place where he'd been made.

Master had no delusions that he was not doing what he'd been sent here to do. But once he'd landed on this place, this place of milk and blood, he'd realized almost at once something that he'd not had in the other realm. He was in control of himself.

"They did not tell us we could think or talk about these things." It had taken him nearly a millennium to figure out how to make the simple stone into something more and use it for his own purposes. The agate, a common enough stone on this place, was easy to find but most importantly, it was perfect for him to mold into what he needed it for. A stone of wealth.

Master had no idea what it was really called by those that knew of some of its properties. It was perfect for communication or used to communicate with the stronger of the soldiers. And once it was inserted into their hearts, it also changed them.

They were subservient before he did this to them but afterwards, it was perfect. They could not just talk to him, give him information, but they could keep him abreast of what was going on. To test his theory when he'd done this to his first adherent, he'd ordered the man to leap from the building. Without hesitation the man had turned, ran to the edge and dove off the building as if he were going to land in a lake of deep blue water. Master had laughed for nearly a week before he tried it again with the same results.

After many trials and mostly errors, he ended up not just changing the men he needed to help him run his empire, but had a group of men that would do as he bid without question. Well, until recently.

Who was doing this? He knew that there was a man. He didn't know his name, but he knew of one man that had been killing his kind for years. Master had met him once, long ago when he'd been on a field of bodies. The time was never clear in his head, and he had a hard time remembering if it was him or someone else, but Master knew that he'd met him before.

Never a great many of them did he manage to kill, a few here and a few there. But whoever this was worked on a higher level than the man had he thought. First of all, there had been a massive killing at the hospital today. One man could not have killed so many so easily. There had to be another army building up somewhere.

Master looked at his leg. The wound was sealed, of course, but the scar was still there. He tried to use his own magic in it, to rid him of the scar. But all it did was burn deeper so that now the scar was black and not pinkish. He'd have to take care to find the wolf's family to make them pay for this. He had no idea how to go about that. He'd never actually drank from the man. But there was a way to simply kill all the shifter wolves and be done with the lot of them. He hated them and anything that didn't comply with what he wanted. And rarely did any of the shifters want to have anything to do with him. Master was going to not just rule but take this place and all that was in it. The humans were going to die.

He lay back on his bed and closed his eyes. Reaching far beyond where he was, Master touched the mind of the man who had helped to create him. The happiness he felt from him made him smile.

"You have killed them all and are bored now, correct?" Master laughed at the long going joke. It truly wasn't funny, but he laughed with him all the same. *"What is it I can do for you? Oh and you should know that Hector's wife left this world for the next. She died as peacefully as she could in her sleep. It was difficult for me to get in there and give her the last of the blood she needed to push her over, but it is done. The child will be next."*

"Hector will need to suffer harshly before we kill him as well. And his blood will go a long way in making more soldiers for us." His ally in the other world told him it would indeed. *"I need to have you give me more of the stone magic. I have lost three of them and without those particular three, I cannot make more."*

That was his greatest fear when he'd had to use the last of his stones, the three that had been taken from him in the fight today. And now, along with the men that carried them, they were gone. And there was only so much of the magic left to make more. He hated the limitations set on him.

"Lost them did you? How did that happen?" He didn't answer, and his ally laughed. *"No matter. I can give you a little more but not enough to make three again. Perhaps you should take better care of your tools, Benton."*

He hated when his given name was used even if it was his middle name. He was glad now that he'd never given him his real name. Things would not have gone so well had he been that stupid. He was Master now, master of the soldiers and adherents that had been created to do his bidding. Instead of correcting him as he'd done before and was ignored, he waited for the man to stop tisking at him.

"There is someone here that destroyed the vessels they were in." That shut him up. *"They not only destroyed the soldiers but all traces of them. I cannot even find their essences. That is where the stones were lost to me. The person, whoever he was, has taken them. It was as if he used the same power on them that you did when we were attacked some years ago."*

His ally had been here to help them set up. The man, whoever he was, had walked in on them and had pulled his weapon. Master remembered now. It had been a long blade that had been covered in blood, the blood of the dead. That alone could kill him, and in the process, it would make him suffer in ways that Master never wanted to think about. It was the only thing that would kill the people from the other realm, the very kind of thing that was killing off Hector's family. The blood of the dead.

"Who? Were you able to find out? When did this...? You have to take me there now. I have to find out who this is." He started cursing, and Master had a moment of pure glee. To have upset the man, that made Master feel very good indeed. "Do you know what this can do to our plans if this person figures it out? Not just my plans but all the other worlds as well?"

"Your plans?" He ignored Master for a moment, and he tried again. "I thought these were our plans. I thought this plan was for us to rule?"

"You know what I mean." He didn't and nearly said so, but the man spoke again. "I shall be there as soon as I can make up excuses. This could not have come at a worse time, Benton."

Master leaned back against the wall he was near. There was something wrong here. He wasn't really sure what it was, but he had a feeling that if he didn't find out soon he'd be back on the other realm in prison. If not dead. This man, his ally, was not one to fuck with. Master figured that he'd have to do something now. Because he was not going to be anyone to fuck with either.

~~~

As Skylar paced around the room, Remy tried to work. She was distracting him, and the longer she was in here, the more he was losing his ability to think. When a stranger came into the room with them, it was all Remy could do not to kill him.

"Hello." The man looked at him, but his eyes were on his Skylar. "I've been sent up to monitor the computers. There are five of us in all, and we're to take shifts."

Skylar nodded, but Remy had had enough. Stepping in front of her, standing between her and the man, he growled low. The man nodded and took a step back.

Remy had just claimed her, and the man seemed to understand.

"I'd like to talk to you." The man sat at the computer and seemed to be setting things up the way he wanted. When he stood again and pulled several of the computer screens from a cabinet, Remy looked at Skylar. She seemed to have forgotten what she'd been saying.

"What is it you need to speak to me about? And the stones not only light up when they're together, but they strobe as well. What do you suppose that means?" Her shrug had him wondering if she was paying any attention to him at all. "Shall we go upstairs?"

"I want you to think of one of the rooms in the house. Any of them. Like...I don't know, think of the library. What color is the second sofa in that room?" He told her he had no idea and frowned when she seemed upset with him. "You have to know. Think. What color is it?"

"Blue. It has a golden pillow on it." He wasn't sure and nodded to her when she asked. "What is this about? You're upset. Tell me."

"Let's go see." He followed her to the room and there it sat. The blue sofa with several gold-colored pillows on it. "It wasn't like this before. See?"

She handed him her cell phone, and he looked at the sofa. In the picture it was maroon with dark blue pillows. The one next to it was a dark green with blue pillows as well. He looked at the picture, then the room twice before handing it back to her.

"You've changed it. I love it." She shook her head. "Then what are we talking about. The couch has been moved or changed. You did it."

"No. I didn't. You did it." She put her cell phone in her back pocket. "Think of something you would like to have to eat. Something small, like some ice cream. Have you had that in a while?"

"No. It was never my favorite. I don't care for it much. But something small? Let me see. How about those cookies...I believe they are called short breads. Do you like them?"

"Not really. But where would you like these cookies to be? I mean in our room? The pantry? Or how about on the kitchen table?" He had no idea what she was going on about and told her the table. "Good. Come on."

She grabbed his hand and nearly dragged him to the kitchen. When he entered behind her, he bumped into her and had to move around her when she seemed frozen in place. But she only had eyes for something in front of her, and he looked too.

"Christ." She nodded and sat down. Remy did as well with the package of shortbread cookies between them. "Did you do that?"

"No. You did it." She nodded when he shook his head. "The house is doing as we need it to do. The bedroom upstairs, I had a thought of mine as a child, the colors were all pinks and golds, but I loved it. As I started to explore the house, the first room I entered was exactly what I'd had as a child. The same with the library and our bedroom."

"What else?" She looked around the room, then back at him. "Tell me, Skylar. What else have you discovered?"

"The house is a good deal bigger than it looks from the outside. I would think if you measured each room and compared it to the outside of the building the difference would be way less than it should be. Then there are the vehicles in the garage." He asked her what garage. "My point exactly. We have not just a garage but several cars in it. There is also a sublevel under it as well as this place. Like several hundred feet below us."

"That's not possible." She only nodded. "That would mean that...I wished for sublevels. With a medical team there. I have no use for them, but the need was there. And in this basement, do you know if there is a tunnel to the garage as well as an outlet far from here?"

"No, but there will be." Remy nodded and got up to pace. The sound of the cookies opening had him turn, and he watched as she ate one. "These are wonderful. I've only been able to afford the cheap ones. These are so much better."

"I have not had any in decades." When she offered him one, he took it. It was buttery and soft with just enough crisp to make him think of fires on a grate. A small woman came into the kitchen just as he was thinking of a cup of tea, and she nodded once before setting a dark kettle on the flame she'd started. "Your name, it's Ann, is it not?"

"You are correct. And you are Rembrandt." Ann didn't turn, but pulled two cups from the cabinet above her head. "I have felt that you were different. I had no idea how so until now. You and she, the missus. You're going to save us all, aren't you?"

"We're going to try." Skylar asked him how he knew the woman's name. "She is the spitting image of the woman who cared for me when I first turned. She was the kindest woman I'd met. She had a daughter too; Catherine was her name. She died in child birth."

Ann turned to him, her hand over her heart, and he knew then that there was a child and her body was swollen with child. Before he could assure her that things had changed and that he would do everything within his power to keep them both, babe and mother, safe, the girl in question came into the room.

"I'm not going to die." Remy shook his head and stood up to offer her is chair. She took it, moving slowly in her ungainly size. "I'm doing well. The doctor assured me that I am."

"You will have the best of care. We will see to it." Remy looked at Skylar, who nodded as well. "No harm shall come to those that are here with us. We might get beaten a bit, but you will be safe. I promise."

The door to the kitchen opened. A man fell into the doorway and lay there looking at them all. Catherine screamed. Holding her belly, she fell to the floor and pulled the man to her body. Remy could only stare at him wondering how he'd gotten here.

"It's the baby's father. We thought him…we were told he was dead." Ann told them and asked him to help the young man up, and he carried him to the elevator. Remy didn't even bother looking at Skylar as she and Catherine entered with him. There had been no elevator there before. He'd bet his life on it.

The man, Jarvis Thomas, lay on the bed as the team worked on him. Catherine stayed for as long as they'd let her, but in the end, she'd been asked to leave the room as well. Remy was told that the man was wolf and once he shifted he'd heal. Nodding, Remy took Skylar's hand and made his way to one of the rooms on the upper floor. It was past time they talked. As soon as they entered what he'd hoped was an office, the room shifted once and settled. Remy only pulled her to him and held on. Things were beyond what he'd ever thought of.

"It will settle once the others are here." He nodded, not knowing why she knew this but didn't care. It was more than he had. "Our magic is making it so that everyone is comfortable. We have a lot to deal with and this will be their only haven for a long time."

"I want no more changes done while we're in the room." Skylar nodded and giggled. "I was in the bathroom when the wall expanded and the shower enlarged. All I had thought of was how much fun it would be to take you against the wall and that it would be a tight fit."

"I love you." He kissed the top of her head and continued to hold her while she leaned into him. "This man, do you think he'll help us? Or…I'd rather he only kept Catherine calm and safe until the baby is born. I don't want anything to happen to any of them."

"We'll keep them safe." She nodded again, and all he could think about was keeping her safe. "The men in the computer room, do you think them to be helpful?"

"I think that anyone that makes it past the barrier is someone we can trust." Remy nodded again. He believed her. He had no idea why, but he had a feeling she was right. Remy held onto her until she pulled back. "It's time for bed, don't you think?"

"Yes," Remy answered her. He was more than ready for bed. Perhaps. He thought that tomorrow would prove to be better, calmer. But as he followed her up the stairs, he had a feeling it wouldn't be. Not for a very long time.

Chapter 9

Hector was standing at the edge of the barrier when she spied him. There was something so profoundly sad that instead of waiting for Remy to come with her, she went to the man. He looked as if he had something in his hands and the closer she got to him, the more afraid she was.

"He will die." Hector held the child she could see now out to her. "He is all I have left in the world, and I don't want to lose him."

Stepping over the barrier, she took the child from his father's hands. Skylar wasn't sure he was going to give him up, but as soon as she touched him, the child looked up at her and smiled. She knew then that she had to do something.

"If he crosses over, I will never see him again." Skylar looked at Hector, then at the child. "You have a team of medical men. I have seen to it that you have the best. Take him to them. Please. If he should die by crossing over, it will be a much less painful death than the one that awaits him at my home."

"His mother, she has died?" Hector sobbed and fell to his knees. The man was crying so hard that he woke the boy in her arms, but only for a moment. "Hector, what are you doing to help him?"

"Everything. I have hired so many doctors to see to him. His mother lost her mind at the end, and she screamed in pain so much that I had to leave. It hurt me to hear her, hurts me more that her son, our child will suffer the same way. I know not what is killing him, and neither do the doctors on our realm." Skylar saw Remy coming with two men dressed in white. She had no idea how he knew, but she was so grateful for his help that she nearly cried herself. Hector watched as his son was taken away. "He did not die."

"No. I'm not sure what you expected or what we did, but we'll do everything in our power to save him." He nodded and looked at her. "Your wife, when did she pass?"

"Yesterday morning. I was with her. Her body was eaten by whatever is taking our son. I don't know what to do now. All I had was these two. What will I do now, Skylar?" She told him she had no idea, but she would help. "There is something that I would ask of you. It is not a huge thing, but something…will you not tell anyone that Ruben is here? I should…I have no idea why, but I think him safer for no one knowing."

"You think someone there is hurting your son?" Skylar looked at Remy when he spoke. She could almost feel his pain and wanted to go to him. But he stood there as hard and as stiff as she'd ever seen him, and she knew he was thinking of his own son. "There are men who you work with. You have them in your mind. Two you trust, but one you do not. Are these men, are they the ones that you fear harming your family?"

"Yes. All of them." Hector stared at the building but said nothing. She wondered what he saw when he looked at it. Skylar wondered if there was a glow about it, like the one she felt when she entered any of the new rooms. "This place, you've made it a home."

"We have. And we have a lot of people here too thanks to you." Hector nodded. He said nothing more but stared at the home when Remy continued. "I should like to speak to you about the stones we've found in the bodies of a few of the adherents. What might you know about them?"

"Stones?" He looked at Remy, but Skylar could see he was having a hard time keeping up with the conversation. "What sort of stones and where are you finding them?"

As Remy told him, Skylar reached into his mind to see what she could find. It was much easier than she'd thought it would be, simply sliding into his head as if she were a part of him. But it took her a few minutes to sort out his grief and guilt to find anything helpful. That was when she came upon the man called Dolin.

He had been here. A good deal over the past weeks. As the building was still moving and shifting, Dolin had been just on the border making notes. Hector had been shadowed as he'd watched him, and he worried about what the man was doing. As she dug deeper, she saw that Hector suspected that Dolin, a onetime good friend, had done something to the people of their realm. Something that was killing them.

Skylar looked for more information. And it seemed that he was telling them, telling Remy everything that he knew. All of it true so far as he knew. But his thoughts, his fears were still there, buried deeply so as not to make himself worry about something as heinous as what he suspected Dolin was doing to them.

"I shall give you all you need. You need only to call to me and I will be here." Remy nodded, then looked at her as Hector continued. "Please, if it is within your power, please save my son. And should something happen to me...should I not return, I should be grateful if you could raise him as your own. Never telling him what a coward I have been."

He looked at her, and she could see that he knew she'd been in his mind. *"It is what I had hoped when I brought my son here to you. I know not what to do about Dolin and the others. I don't even know what they hope to gain by killing us all."*

"I don't either, but we'll try to find out." He nodded once and shook Remy's hand. Her he hugged to him. "Take care. And if you need us, just come here. I'll have someone watching for you at all times."

"I will." Skylar had a feeling he wouldn't be back, not like this. If and when he returned, it would be more businesslike. She knew for whatever reason no one would ever know he was here. After telling Remy goodbye, he left them. Skylar looked at the soldiers around them.

"They're afraid of us. And of this place. See how far they stay from the boundaries?" When he didn't answer her, she looked at him. All she could think of was the things he'd done to her last night and again this morning.

"I want you." Nodding, she let him pick her up. His shoulder in her belly had her bouncing up and down as he ran to the house. In short order they were in their room and naked, the wall behind her was pressing into her back as he was her front. "Christ, do you have any idea how much I want to taste every part of you?"

"Yes. Please. Do it." He let her down and stepped back. His cock was straining from his body and leaking at the tip. Wrapping her fingers around him, she felt his need like it was hers. Hell, it truly was as bad as hers. "I'm going to suck on you until you come down my throat."

"All right." Smiling at his chocked out response, she licked him from tip to root when she dropped in front of him. "Skylar, you're going to have me coming quickly if you keep that up."

"That's the plan." Cupping his balls had him rocking into her mouth, and she held him with her fist as she licked him around and around with her tongue. He was holding onto the wall behind her now, his cock sliding in and out of her mouth like he had her pussy only hours before.

Running her hands over his tat at his leg, she felt the warmth of the magic. Her own body stirred when he curled his fingers into her hair and held her tightly against him. He was fucking her harder now, his cock sliding past the tight muscles of her throat every time.

She knew when he was going to come. His balls were heavy with his cum, his body hard with the strain of holding back. When Skylar stretched her hand up and pinched his nipple, he nearly knocked her over with his cock. The feel of his cum spraying now the back of her throat had her sliding her fingers into her pussy and bringing herself to a quick satisfying release.

Remy leaned heavily against the wall now. His head buried in the crock of his arm, and his cock, still hard, was near her mouth. When she licked him, cleaning him up, he took a step back and picked her up.

"My turn." He helped her to the bed. And after laying her just the way he wanted her, he sat down on the floor between her legs and pulled her to the very edge of the mattress. "I love feeding from you this way. Not just when you let me bite you and I take what I need but your juices give me more than I can explain to you. And you come so prettily that I want to keep you coming all the time."

"I know what you mean. When you come down my throat, it's all I can do not to beg you to do it again and again." His tongue made its way from her gate to her clit. And then he played with her with his tongue before he sucked her into his mouth. "Remy."

He teased her over and over. Bringing her to the edge several times only to keep her from falling. Her body was covered in sweat. Her need was so close that she knew that when he let her come, and she hoped it would be soon, that she was going to bring the house down around them. Suddenly, he was gone and she sat up, her body on fire for him.

"Come to the chair for me. I want to fuck you while you bend over it. Putting that pretty ass of yours there where I can see it." Nodding, she staggered to a standing position only to have him scoop her up and help her. Skylar was trembling with need, and when she bent over, her thighs spread out for him, she screamed out another fast, hard climax. Then he slapped her ass.

"I've been dying to see you all pink from my hand." His hand came down again, and she panted. "You respond so well to me spanking you that it makes me wonder what you would do if I tied you to the bed."

Her body responded to his words as if he had her there now. The climax that ripped from her took her breath away and had her screaming out his name. When she stood there, ready for whatever he did to her, she knew that he was going to tie her up. When she was moved to the middle of the room and her arms lifted, she knew that Remy had modified the room for this.

Her legs were spread wide, as wide as her arms. She stood there, naked and aching for him, when he came up behind her. His cock played between her legs but never entered her as he cupped her breasts, tugging hard on her nipples until she was sobbing.

"Come for me, Skylar. Come while I think about how I'm going to fuck you this way." He slid his fingers down her belly to her pussy and into her pussy. She rode his fingers hard while he toyed with her nipples with his other hand. "Come now."

Her body seemed to freeze for several seconds. Her heart stopped beating, her breath, caught somewhere in her throat, seemed to clog her thinking as well. She let go, her body giving over to the incredible pleasure that was promised to her. She screamed over and over as she came, saying Remy's name like a litany until she was weak from it.

He entered her hard, his hand at her waist as he held her tight to his body. It was strange to have him in her this way, the way he held her upright and filled her too. When his teeth grazed over her shoulder, making her blood feel like it was boiling, she knew that when he bit her, sank his fang into her, she was going to come with him. And this climax would pale when compared to all the others he'd given her.

"I'm coming," he cried out as he sank into her flesh. His mouth, like his cock, took her hard, fast and had her coming with him. As she soared up again, this time the peak just out of her reach, Remy slid his fingers into her pussy with his cock and it threw her over. Skylar couldn't even scream this time. Her entire body was too busy trying to stay whole. Then…just like that, everything went black.

~~~

Remy lay beside her. He had meant only to make love to her then talk. They had both been so busy that there was little time for anything but work and sleep. And even that was low on their priority list. As soon as they were in this room, they were naked and he was inside of her in some way. Smiling, he thought of all the ways he'd been inside this woman.

"You look like you've been given an early present." He shook his head and then held her to him as she yawned. "How long have you been here with me? The reason I ask is I was thinking about young Ruben."

"He is still being observed. Weston said that he believes the boy to be poisoned. And until he finds out with what, he's afraid to try much to get him better." It made sense, he supposed, but the boy was dying and they all knew it. "I told him to call us as soon as there was any change."

"We can't let him die." Remy nodded, holding her. He didn't want the youngster to die either, but there was little known about his kind. "I was in Hector's mind. He thinks that Dolin and two other men, men by the name of Frank and Ward, are killing their people. If it's poison, we'll have to figure out how they're getting it."

"It will have to be in something that is common for them all. Did you notice that Hector looks ill as well? I wonder if he brought the boy here because he knew his time was coming to an end as well." Skylar sat up, then got out of the bed. As he watched her, she spread her wings out and stretched. Seeing her naked like this made his cock stir, but he knew that she had to do this or hurt. He had done the same thing before coming to find her this morning.

"I've been thinking about the stones." He nodded. It was all he thought about as well. "The heart that you gave to Weston, did he tell you what he found?"

"He said there was a chamber in it to hold a stone. And it wasn't in the others, the malefactor that we'd brought them last night didn't have one anyway." She nodded, and her wings folded into her body. Remy was sure she'd not even realized she'd done it, but when she turned back to him, she was dressed. "Are you planning to go out?"

"I need to kill something." Nodding, he stood up. He knew the feeling well. But if she thought to leave him alone, he was going to tell her differently. "There was some talk of a building on the other side of town. A large one, not like this, but big."

"I have heard that too." They'd been called out twice last night and only just diverted a large conversion by having the programs on the computers to help them. "We need to see if we can talk to one of the malefactors. I know that we cannot bring them here, but perhaps we can have a conversation with one while we are out."

At the bottom of the stairs was Davis. He looked ready to do some serious battle. And when Remy told him they were going out, he asked to join them. The man looked like he had been up all night, and he asked him about it.

"That boy. Bothers me on all sorts of levels to know that he's ill like that. What it must have cost Hector to give him over to us." Remy nodded. "Anyway, I need to get out too. And I was just down in the command center when that guy, Jake Roman, said that there was a sort of gathering not far from that building that was on our radar last night."

Before they left the building, Remy went to check on both Ruben and Jarvis. Jarvis was healed but still resting. Weston asked for him not to be wakened, as he'd had a bad night as well. But he did tell Remy that the younger man wanted to talk to him. Then they went to see Ruben.

"I have several things to tell you before I give you what I know or really don't know about the boy. First, the blood that was in the first heart you gave me is not the boy's blood type. Skylar had me run that first off. She said that Hector thought that it was his blood poisoning the child." Remy asked him if that was all he'd found with the blood. "No. As a matter of fact, I have good news about that. Skylar also said that Hector was sure he'd created these monsters by putting his blood in the vials when they made them. His DNA, or at least that of the boy, is not in the monsters' blood. Not any markers at all. Whoever did this, it wasn't him."

"He's not like them." The doctor shook his head smiling. "So he could come here too. I mean, if the boy could cross over, he might be safer here."

"Not necessarily. The child hasn't yet come to his age yet. Like most shifters, I'm assuming that there is a time in their life when they become whatever their parent is. I don't know a lot about their kind, so I'm going on what I am. Which is a wolf. This boy, like any that I might have, is just a human. A stronger and healthier human despite his illness, but..." He looked down at the kid. "Had a regular human gotten poisoned with what this child has been he'd have died long ago. The only thing keeping him going is the fact that his parents are not human. I would think that whatever he's being fed or given is a slow process. Being here, it might just save his life if we can give him what he needs."

"And what might that be?" Weston said he had no idea right now. "What do you need from me? Whatever it is, we can get it for you."

"A live soldier or adherent would be great. I know that that might be impossible, but…" He looked around the clinic before looking back at him. Remy would do whatever it took to make this place perfect for the man. He'd done so much for them already. "This is the most well equipped place I've ever…hell, Remy, this place is better than most hospitals. What I could use here is some help. A few nurses, another doctor to bounce ideas off of. I know it's a lot, and you've given me more than I could ever hope for, but—"

"I'll get it." Nodding, the man only smiled at him. "Do you doubt me? Trust me when I say that Skylar and I will make sure you have anything and everything you need. Including your live specimens. Just…have a bag ready to go when we come for you. As you have said, they can't come here alive, but we can have them for you to work on somewhere else."

"I'll do that." Remy left him then and found the others in the kitchen. Ann was making a sandwich for Davis, and the man was flirting with her. As soon as they were out in the car, Remy asked him about wings.

"I don't have any. Should I?" Davis looked at Skylar, then him. "You have them. Damn. I suppose you'd need them more than me. Being in charge and all. And if that's a perk to being in charge, then you can have the job. Not worth the worry. I love working with you guys, but I don't think I'm cut out for being boss."

Remy glanced at Skylar. They had done a little talking last night and they were going to need for Davis to be in charge at some point. With twelve more men coming their way, it would be difficult for them to be spread out that thinly.

He told them what the doctor had said as Davis drove them to the place where they'd been told to go. "From what I understand, having a live specimen means he could get a better understanding of a lot of things. Not just his blood but, heart, lungs, and his bone structure."

"I can see that. The two that we've brought him have been a little beaten up. Having a whole person could tell him a lot of things that a dead one would not. And I can make sure that whatever he needs to know, the malefactor answers him." Skylar grinned at him. "I'm getting very good at this whole holding and answering crap."

She was too. Just the other day she'd gotten Ann to tell her the real reason she and her granddaughter were here. While it did have a great deal to do with Ann's husband, it wasn't all of it. She was also being hunted by some very nasty people her husband had sold her to. That guy was going to die as soon as Remy found him. And it wouldn't be a quick one either.

"He's going to need a lab. We can't be taking them things with us to the compound. Where is he going to…?" Remy started to tell him that he would bring what he needed when Davis laughed. "We could take over one of them hospitals that is now flunked out. Just to do offsite work on. There are a number of them not far from here. And with you guys having a means to get there quickly, we could simply buy one and use it like a sort of lab."

"What an amazing idea." Skylar looked at him and appeared so embarrassed that he had to smile. "Do you think we can afford that? I mean, I know that most cities will sell cheap just to get it off their books, but I have no idea what the going rate is."

"I'm sure we can. But having it in our name might be tricky." She nodded, and he wondered what was going on in her brilliant mind when a thought occurred to him. "I suppose we could simply just take it. I mean, we have the ability to not have people know where we are if we don't want them to."

It was perfect so far as they could see. Move in without anyone knowing. Have the lab set up…Remy wondered if the magic that they had at their home would transfer to somewhere else, but didn't voice that part. He was happy to use any means they could get their hands on to make this war a little less one sided. Especially when it was weighing on the side of the bad guys.

Chapter 10

Master looked around the room. There were less than he'd hoped for on this first meeting, but they were still working on the problems of getting more soldiers to work with them. They'd had another seven kill themselves today. That was a total of two dozen in the last week. Not good odds, he thought, since they'd only managed to convert five dozen humans counting them.

"Master, it is time." Master nodded at the man next to him. He had no idea what his name was and as with all of the soldiers and adherents, they all really did look exactly alike. As the man sat next to him, Master glanced over at the placard that had been place before everyone but him. Sam was all it said.

He'd refused to have one put in front of him. If anyone didn't know him by now, he figured they should be dead. As he took another look around the room, he wondered how many of the men and women there even had a clue what they were supposed to be doing. Doubtful. If they did, they would have filled this room, not merely standing room only. The five hundred or so that milled about the room was far from the army that they'd need soon. Standing up, the room grew quiet.

"I am here to welcome you to my fold." He stretched out his hands in welcome, but no one said a word. "I am Master to you all. And the reason I am calling this meeting tonight is because there have been some questions about what—"

"I don't want to kill no one." The person in the back spoke loudly and no matter how hard he tried, Master could not see him. Then another spoke. "My wife died because she didn't want to be this way and you want me to do this to others? Why the hell should I make them as miserable as I am?"

"You were nearly dead when we converted you. Would you have rather we let you die?" The man nodded. "I see. Well, we can take care of that now."

Nodding once, Sam got up and went to the man. Surprisingly, he stood there waiting. As the sea of people parted to let them come together, Master waited for someone to protest. But all they did was watch as Sam rammed a pike into the man's chest and killed him.

"Is there anyone else who would like to join him?" No one moved and Master had a moment of fear. There was a feeling in the room, not just from a few of the people but nearly all of them that he was evil. As he opened his mouth to speak again, three more people stepped to the front of the room just in his vison and stood there. "You have something to say?"

"Yeah." The noise just outside of the room had them all turning. There were screams and sounds of things being thrown against the building, but no one came in. Master found himself looking for an exit. Some way for him to escape should whoever was out there breach the door. But before he could make good on it, the doors opened all around the room, and Master felt sweat roll down his back.

The man who walked in was huge. Bigger than anyone he'd ever encountered. He backed up, but the man lifted his hand and Master could not move. Then he spread his wings. Master could only stare at him as he continued to advance to him. Then…a woman? There was a woman just behind him. Her wings were wide as well, but instead of smiling—as the man was—she was standing there with her arms crossed over her breast, and her face looked as if she would kill anyone who came near her.

"What is the meaning of this?" Sam stood up as he spoke, his body poised to leap over the table he sat at when he was suddenly gone. Master looked at the space where he'd been and then back at the man.

"Having a meeting?" Master nodded. And then felt foolish. "That's nice of you to bring all these dead men to us. I'm assuming you think you're in charge here."

"I am. I am Master." The man grinned. "What are you? And why do you dare come into my home without an invitation?"

"Home?" The man looked back at the woman, then at him again. "Not much of a home if you asked me. I don't know why, but I expected something more grandiose for someone calling himself 'master.'"

"We are gathering our forces to kill the humans." Master snapped his mouth closed. He had no idea why he was telling this man this, but he found that he could not lie. "Go away and we will fight another time."

"No." Someone, one of his soldiers, was moving toward the man as he spoke. Master was so proud of the man that he decided to make him an adherent as soon as this was over. But before he could touch the big man, the woman stepped forward and cut him in half. Literally. As his body lay there in the dark blood, the sword she had in her hands disappeared into her pants. The man cleared his throat.

"What are you doing here?" Master tried to move again and cried out at the pain it caused him. "You have no rights here. This is a meeting to boost the men into killing more humans. You being here is not helping."

"Who do you work for?" Master felt the compulsion. It was so strong that he hurt with it. The man sat in one of the few empty chairs as he continued. "We know that you aren't smart enough to have done this on your own. We also know that for as much as you think you're going to destroy the humans here, we're not going to let that happen. So, my question to you is, who do you work for?"

"I don't know what you mean." It cost him to lie to the man. Pain ran over his body like a storm did, hot rain spilling over his body until he nearly crumbled under the weight of it. "There is no one in charge but me."

Master was taken to his knees. He wasn't sure if he'd fallen from the intense pain or someone had hit him. The man, a large man, stood over him with a sword at the back of his neck and held him there. He could only see his boots, but even those were bigger than anything he'd ever seen.

"Now, we're going to do this again. Who do you work for?" Master felt the blood spill from his nose and ears. It dripped onto the floor in front of him, as blue as the waters of his home realm. "The man's name and I will end your suffering."

"You think you're going to kill me?" The man laughed, as did the man holding him there. "I am Master. I will rule."

"Not so long as I'm alive you won't." Master had a few things he wanted to say to the man. One of which was he could die now and Master would be thrilled. But he doubted that he'd find any humor in it. Instead, the blade at is neck dug deeper into him.

"I know not his name." He didn't know it. He'd been Lord when he'd been on the realm and since then he'd only called him ally. "He does not come here unless necessary. I rule here. And will when this plan of ours is complete."

The touch to his head had him screaming. It wasn't a gentle search of his mind but a full-out rape of it. Master knew it was the woman too. Her boots, much smaller than the man's were, suddenly in front of him, standing in the blood that still poured from his head.

No one said anything as she did her worst to him. There were noises, a great many of them. And he knew, for whatever reason they thought they had, that his soldiers were being destroyed. When his head was jerked upright, he looked into the most terrifying eyes he'd ever seen. The woman looked like death herself.

"He doesn't know his name." The man asked a question he was sure, but Master was in too much pain to try and figure it out. "No, he only knows that he is to gather a fold. He is paid by magic, and the funds that he has are gone before the end of his day."

"I have expenses." He did too. There was an image to uphold as ruler of this world and he was amassing his wealth in items, not saving his money for later. He really had very little to show for his purchases, but he was happy with the car he had as well as the jewelry. "I demand that you let me go."

He was suddenly free. As he fell back on his ass, he had a chance to look around the room. They had not killed his soldiers but had chained them together. Master started to stand to demand…he had no idea what he would have demanded, but the woman shoved him back on his ass.

"I know what he looks like." The threat, because there was no doubt that was what it was, was said in a low cold voice. "I also know that he's not going to be happy with the results of today. You are going to be in hot water with him when we leave here."

"You're not going to kill me?" His relief was so profound that he wanted to crawl to her on his knees and kiss her feet. But she seemed to know and took several steps back. The man at his right, the one with the blade, laughed. "You would not think this so funny if you were at her mercy."

"No shit." Master looked at her. Then, she made her way to the man sitting in the front row. When he stood up, there was a quiet that went around the room that made Master think of the calm before the storm. He watched them both as they moved to his chained men. That was when he noticed the other man.

"Which do you want?" Master thought the large man spoke to him, but it was the newcomer that he spoke to. "And if you tell me you want that shit up there, I'm sorry, but he's going to live for a bit longer. I need him for something else."

Master was thrilled to know he was set to live. He didn't care what they told him to do, not that he'd do any of it, but he would live. And gather an army against these people. When the woman turned to him and winked,

Master had a feeling she knew just what he had been thinking.

"I would like two of the soldiers and however many adherents there are. That way I can have a look at the stones too." Master started to stand, but the blade was suddenly quivering between his legs. He didn't use his cock for anything anymore, but the thought of it being removed this way had it shrivel more to his body. He looked up at the man who had stopped him from moving.

"I'll take great pleasure in having my ass torn up by that man if I can kill you. So just so we're both on the same page, I will cut your head from your body and piss down your neck if you so much as move your finger toward them." Master nodded. "I almost want you to try. Almost. I'd like nothing more than to fucking tear you apart."

"I have done nothing to you." The man growled. "Those people either. But if you should like to come and work for me, I will make you my second and no one will ever replace you. Just say the word."

Master felt his neck snap back. His eyes and nose felt as if a large log had been smashed into him as he fell backward. As soon as his head hit the floor behind him, the man with the blade appeared above him, and all Master managed to get out was *no* before everything went black.

~~~

Skylar watched Weston. The man was taking his time, but she wasn't worried about that so much as what the plan was for the guy on the podium. Glancing his way again, she wasn't surprised to see him still out. Davis had said he'd never been so mad in his life. When Remy said her name, she looked at him.

"They...some of them want to die." She nodded. There was something so very sad about this group of people. "Why would someone do this to them when they don't want it?"

She didn't point out that both of them had been changed without their permission, but he seemed to understand. As he walked to the line of men and women again, she sat on the chair closest to her. One of the men stared openly at her but said nothing. Then it occurred to her that he might not be able to speak.

Walking to him had several of the people reach out to her. They never touched her, but she could see that they would if they thought they could get by with it. When the man that had stared at her nodded, she sat down in another chair and looked up at him.

"You're going to die. You know that, don't you?" He nodded and looked away, then back. "There is no way we can leave you here. You're only set for one thing and that's to convert humans."

He nodded and then put out his hands. She had no idea if it was a good idea or not, but she touched her hand to his. The connection was slight, but she could read his thoughts like he was talking to her.

"I wish only to join my wife and grandchild." She nodded as he continued. *"They were killed in the same accident that nearly killed me. This thing pulled me from her arms, my wife of nearly fifty years, as I begged to join her."*

"You have to be near death for them to convert you. We've only just found this out." She looked at him and realized that he'd not been changed for long. "When did your family die? And how did you know about coming here?"

"*Today. Not long ago.*" He looked around before speaking again. "*We all knew to come here. There was like this...beacon in my head to come here. Not all of us, mind you, but the ones that are close. I was...my body was close enough that I could —* "

His body stiffened, and she could see the change taking him a little at a time. When he dropped to his knees, she knew that it was only a matter of minutes before he would no longer be human enough to talk to her.

"The man there, at the podium. Had you met him before today?" He shook his head as another pain took him. "What color was the person who bit you? Faded or was he blue?"

The scream that spilled from his mouth was a word. "Faded" was drawn out into a long two syllable word until she saw that he'd lost his humanity. As he straightened up and snarled at her, she could see that he was fully whatever had made him. And he would likely kill her if given half a chance. When she put out her arm, the one with the tats all the way up it, the man shied away, but it was too late. Skylar let her magic go, and the man incinerated in seconds.

There were a total of fifty-four men and women. Nine of them were blue, and the rest were varying shades of nothing to pale faded color. Each of them were dressed and looked the same. None of them spoke to them, not even the blue guys, nor the adherents, even though they knew that they could.

"Weston took three of the adherents and two of the soldiers. Davis is helping him put them in the van." She'd gone back to the house to get Weston when they realized there were more subjects here than they'd thought there would be. Remy said her name before he continued. "We have to kill them all. If we leave them, there will be untold number of people that they kill or change."

"I know that." She looked up at the one that called himself master. "His name is Benton. Nothing more. He and about a dozen others were brought here just like Hector told us. Benton is supposed to be the one to gather the fold as they call them."

"I wonder if we can use him as a bargaining chip. Sort of bring out the man who is in charge." Skylar shook his head. "Honey, the man has killed so many people. We can't just let him go."

"I know that. And that's not really what I meant. Benton thinks that whoever this person is that he works for is going to double-cross him. And so you know, whoever this man is, he's the one that killed Hector's wife and is murdering his child. It's blood. The blood of the dead. It's deadly to them in a slow and painful way."

"Did you happen to find out what can cure this?" She shook her head. "Well, we know more now than we did before. And now that Weston has his subjects, perhaps we can learn more."

The men and women tied together were hissing and snarling at them. It was well past time to take care of them, and she didn't even feel bad for what they had to do. So far as she was feeling, these people were already dead. She was just there to finish the job.

When Remy moved up behind her, she put out her arm. Since the first day, she'd gotten much better at what she had to do, and she pointed her arm at the monsters. As soon as his arm touched her, the power between them became hot. Almost unbearably hot. And the people seemed to know what was coming. The screaming started almost immediately, and their combined power cut it off just as quickly.

As she pulled back on her power, she felt a renewed sense of energy. Before when they'd practiced, she felt drained, like she could sleep for a week. Now...right now she felt as good as she'd ever felt, and her body seemed to hum with it. Turning in his arms, she looked at Remy. He too looked good. Good enough to eat was all she could think about.

"I need you." Nodding, she let him drag her out of the building. They still had to deal with Benton, but right now if he didn't come inside of her, she felt as if she might die. As soon as they were out, he stretched out his wings. Skylar let hers go as well, and she joined him in the sky. They were at their home in seconds and naked. Skylar took his mouth even as he wrapped her into his wings and held her.

His cock was hard. The tip of it so purple that she wanted to take it into her mouth and see if she could taste the blood pooled there. But Remy picked her up and pulled her down on his cock. She was riding him even as he took her to the wall.

Their wings were touching, and she could feel every emotion, every thought that ran through his mind. When she put an image of him coming, his head thrown back, she knew that he could see it.

"I want you to come hard." She nodded knowing there was no way for her not to come when he was inside of her. "Come with me, love. Come now."

Her body bowed back as she screamed out her release. Remy didn't stop pounding her even as took her throat. The bite, deep and hard, brought her again and when he offered her his wrist, she took it the same way. His climax had him biting her again, her breast, and her shoulder until she felt blood pour from the wounds. When he rubbed it into her body, sucking it off her like he was feasting, Skylar came again, and bit him in the throat.

Feeding him like this, all she could think of was how much she loved him. When she finished, never taking all that much anyway, she leaned back against the wall and looked at him. Remy sealed the several wounds he'd given her and held her to him. Their wings, still full fluttered, slightly when he turned them to the bed.

"We can't." Before he could say anything else, she reminded him that they had left Benton at the building. "I would love nothing more than to crawl into that bed and sleep but right now, we have to deal with that asshole."

"You're right." As he backed from her, his wings curled against his body. She stretched hers until she felt like she could do the same but watched as he paced the room. She asked him what he was thinking. "What if we just left him there? I mean, what if he goes back to this bastard and we figure out who he works for."

"I guess, but won't they just start up somewhere else?" He said he didn't know. "I guess knowing who we're dealing with will help. But we'd have to get there now. I'm betting he has some way of talking to this person that doesn't use a phone."

As they took to the skies again, Skylar thought of all the things that had been going on. In such a short amount of time, she'd lost her job, found a lover, changed into something with magic, and had wings. She almost forgot the tats. Those had come in handy today as well. And Davis.

He had a sword. It was long and curved, and she had a feeling it was something that he was used to using in his former life. Because when he had needed it, he used it like he was comfortable with it, not like she was with the guns.

When the building was within their sight, they both moved into the shadows of it to watch. Remy had gone in quietly to see if Benton was still there, and when he came out and gave her the thumbs up, she was actually disappointed. If he was gone, they'd have nothing else to work on tonight. But with him there, they had to wait. Or take him with them. Either way, so long as he was out, there wasn't much they could do. But wait. Not one of her better traits.

Chapter 11

Hector listened to the man twice. There was no way what he was telling him was true. He knew this as surely as he was sitting here. His son was not dead.

"When did you say this happened?" Dolin put his hand on his shoulder when he asked. "I mean, you've already told me no doubt, but I just…when?"

"Yesterday. While you were out." He'd been on earth dealing with the malefactor that had been in charge. After several hours of waiting for someone to show up and claim him, Rembrandt and Skylar had called him. Hector had also found out that his son was being poisoned just as he'd thought. But by who, he still didn't know. Until now.

"He didn't suffer as your poor wife did. He simply went to sleep as he had been doing a lot lately. I…I'm sorry, Hector, but I thought I'd be doing you a favor by having his body taken care of right away." Hector nodded. He wasn't sure what was going on right now. "I had the nurse take him in his blanket to the incinerator."

Who had been taken there, he wondered, and why? The nurse, loyal only to his wife, had done this. But now, there was no way he could talk to her without Dolin present. She had been sent away, it seemed. Her services no longer needed. Hector got up to pace.

"He's all I had in the world." Stalling, he tried to think what to do. Should he demand the truth? Had it been a mistake? Did Dolin really believe that Ruben was dead and truly offered him condolences? As Hector continued to pace, he let his mind settle by thinking of something else. The malefactor.

But to do this, he had to do just what Rembrandt told him to do. Be surprised at the information as he imparted it, yet pissed off. He had wanted to practice, but Skylar assured him that he shouldn't sound like he was reading a script, but that he was being off-handed about it.

"I was in the other realm. They caught a malefactor that thinks he's in charge." He didn't bother looking at Dolin but continued to pace. "To think that I could have been here and not there during my son's last moments. And the man isn't speaking, so I wasted all their time."

"They caught one, did they?" Hector nodded, not slowing his pace. The harder he tried not to think of his child, the more he did. Tears of frustration fell from his eyes as he thought of how useless he'd been to his helpers. "There, there, Hector. Your son is in a better place. Much better. But tell me about this malefactor. Is he one of the newer ones or something else?"

"I didn't really think about it." He thought for a few seconds, giving Dolin the illusion that he was trying to remember. "Blue. Dark blue, I think. And he spoke. I guess Rembrandt has figured out that the blue ones can speak."

"Speak? But you said that he didn't talk. Which is it, man?" Dolin must have realized how upset he sounded and stood up. "I'm sorry. All I can think about is how you were away dealing with this when your son needed you. You should have called me. Or better yet, had Rembrandt call me. That's a thought. Why not have him deal with me on this? I can take care of it while you have time to grieve."

"I'm not going to sit around here and think about Ruben when the person who murdered all those people is out there. I mean, what if this person isn't the one? He might know who it was. Then we can end this once and for all." Dolin nodded, but there was a spark of anger on his face. Hector had known this man nearly all his adult life and knew when he was angered or not. "I'm thinking…there is nothing left for me here. I think I shall lend them my help and go to stay on the earth. There are only memories—"

"No." Hector took a step back from the venom in Dolin's voice. He took several deep breaths as if he were trying to control himself. "No. As I have said, I'll take care of it from now on. You rest. Take care that you don't get sick as well. Here, let me make you a drink."

Hector sat down on his couch. A drink. A drink. It swirled around in his mind over and over until he was sick with it. Weston had told him that Ruben had been poisoned with blood. The blood of the dead. As Dolin came toward him with the glass of amber liquid, Hector wondered what he'd given his son to slowly kill him. When the glass was held out to him, it was all he could do not to slap it away. Instead, he took it and held it in his hand. He stared into the glass as if it had all the answers. Which he supposed it did.

"Ruben would have been ten this year. And Margo and I were planning such a party for him. There would have been all his friends. Your children, of course. And then we were going to take a trip. A long one." Dolin sat across from him and pushed the glass to his body. "What am I going to do, Dolin? I have nothing left."

"You have me as your friend. And I'll take care of you. Drink the drink, Hector. You'll feel better." Nodding, he stood up with the glass still in his hand. "Where are you going? Not to earth again, are you? Hector, I must insist that you drink the wine and then go straight to bed."

"Yes. I will." Taking the glass to his mouth, Hector closed his mouth so that nothing entered his mouth. Then he smiled at his friend as he wiped the moisture from his mouth. "I shall go to bed now. Then I'll finish this off and sleep."

Dolin was nodding and helping him to his room. "There you go. Have a nice nap and you'll feel so much better in the morning. I know I will knowing that you're resting."

As soon as he was at his door, Hector turned and smiled at his friend. "Thank you for all that you've done for my family. You don't know what having a friend like you has done for me."

"Nothing to it. I know that you'd do the same for me. Now. Drink up and rest. It will be the best thing for you." Hector entered his room and closed the door. He'd had a feeling that Dolin was going to join him in the room, but short of knocking down the door, he wasn't coming in. Hector put the glass on the dresser and backed away from it.

Hector thought about all the things he had to do. Getting this to Weston and Rembrandt was a priority, but how to get there was proving to be hard to do. He could transport himself there, but he couldn't take the glass with him. It would disappear along with the few pieces of jewelry he had on only to be left behind until he returned. He'd have to bring him here.

But he had to hide the glass. Where? Looking around the room, he tried to think. There had to be one place, just the one that Dolin would never look. Going to his bathroom, he searched there for a few minutes before it occurred to him. He reached under the counter for his wife's things.

It hurt him in ways that he couldn't think around. She was gone. Never to speak to him again, never to give him a hug. Margo gave the best of hugs. Putting the glass into the box of tampons, he held it to his heart for several seconds just sobbing. Putting it back under the sink, he willed himself to Rembrandt.

~~~

Skylar was in the yard just stretching her wings when she felt the stir in the air. Tucking them tight again her, she looked around to see Hector. He looked...she wanted to say crazed, but that wasn't quite it. But the closer she got to him, the more she could see that he was indeed a little off. Before she could ask him, however, he started speaking quickly.

"He said he was dead. Not that he'd know anything about it but he's not dead, is he?" Without really knowing who he was talking about, she told him his son was holding his own. "I knew it. He lied to me. Not for the...I need you to come with me. It might work, but I have no idea. If it works, I'll know. You'll know too. But you have to come with me."

"Where?" As soon as she stepped over the boundary, she felt the air rush around her. Closing her eyes so she wouldn't be sick, she held tight to the hand that had hers.

There was no time to be afraid, but she was slightly dizzy when she opened her eyes again.

The room was huge and she could see right away that it was a bedroom. Looking at Hector, she nearly hit him when he started talking again. This time it was more disjointed than before.

"I think he killed my wife. Why would he do that? Not that it matters why, I suppose, but he did to it. And to try and kill my son? Why?" She wanted to interrupt him to get some answers, but he moved out of the bedroom to another, then back with a box of tampons. "Can you take this back with you? I need to see...do you have anything on you that came with you? Keys? Maybe...a ring?"

"I have my watch." She showed it to him and he laughed manically. "You're scaring me, Hector. What's going on?"

"He gave this to me to drink." Skylar eyed the box, then looked at Hector. Surely the man was over the edge. "Not this. I'm sorry. I'm so afraid. Here, he gave me this."

The glass was filled with a dark amber liquid. She didn't reach for it and since he didn't offer it up again, she only stared. When he didn't seem inclined to give her anything else to help her, she asked him.

"Perhaps we should start over. Like who gave you this? And why did you come to get me? And while we're on that subject, where the hell am I?" He grinned. It wasn't as insane looking, but it was still a little off. "Hector?"

"My home. This is my home. My wife...she and I lived here with Ruben. But now...I don't want to live here any longer. There are too many horrific memories that black out the good ones." He finally put out the glass. "Dolin gave me this today, just a few minutes ago with the strict orders to drink it down and go to bed. I think…I'm pretty sure that it's nearly all dead blood. And if I were to drink it, I'd be dead too."

"You said he told you your son was gone. He isn't by the way, but why would he say that?" Hector sat down still holding the box of tampons and the glass. "And you think he's trying to kill you now."

"Yes. Especially after yesterday. I think…I have known for a while that Dolin wasn't really on the up and up. But to know that he lied to me about the blood. I have thought all this time that I was the one that caused all this." He looked up at her. "This glass might be the proof I need. I'm not sure what I'd do with it, but I'll have it. He murdered my wife. Tried to murder my only child. I don't understand that."

"Come on. Let's get back. Remy is more than likely freaking the fuck out." He stood up and put his hand on hers. "Hector, we'll figure this out. I swear to you we will."

"I know you will." Before she could say anything else, she was standing in the same place she'd been before he'd yanked her away. Only this time Remy and Davis were there. And neither of them were very happy.

"I can explain." The fist came out and caught poor Hector in the face. He was falling backwards when she grabbed for the glass. She only just managed to catch it up before all of it spilled. Skylar turned on Remy, who had hit him. "You overgrown asshole. What the fuck is wrong with you?"

"He took you." She glared at him and he took a step back. "What the hell was I supposed to think when I come out here to work out with you and see you being taken away by him?"

"You would think, 'hum, there must be something important going on. Perhaps I should ask questions before I ruin everything.' That's what a normal person would do." He said something and her temper snapped. "What the fuck did you just say to me?"

"I said I'm not normal when it comes to you." That had her mouth snapping shut. "You make me crazy with lust, drive me insane with my love for you, and when you're not safe, or what I think is safe, I go a little shit headed."

"You did do that." Hector cleared his throat, and she looked down at him, just remembering what was going on. Helping him to his feet, she handed the glass to Remy. "Don't drink it. It's evidence."

Hector was still standing on the outside of the boundaries when she turned to talk to him. She'd forgotten that he couldn't cross over. But then that was before she'd figured something out.

"If I let you over, will you promise to behave yourself and not piss me off?" He looked at Remy, then at her again. "I can do that. We can. Remy and I make our own sort of rules in this domain."

"I don't know if I cannot piss you off. You are very…strong minded." She grinned at him and watched as he put his foot forward. "If I should die, will you do as I have asked you about Ruben?"

"Yes. But you won't die. And I'm thinking that once you cross over, you'll not be found by Dolin or anyone else that would cause you harm." He nodded but still hesitated. "Hector, your son is awake. He's still very weak, but he had his eyes open yesterday."

"You would not lie to me, would you?" She shook her head. "I should very much like to see him. I miss him so terribly much."

"Then come over." There were so many malefactors around them that she wanted to kill them all. But right now, it was more important that Hector was safe. Skylar had no idea why his safety was so important to her, especially after all he'd done to them. But she waited.

His foot crossed the line first. She could tell that he was waiting for some sort of pain if not instant death, but he looked at her and there was relief there. When his foot touched the earth, then the other, she knew that he was as free as he'd ever been. As they moved forward to the building, she thought about where he would stay now that he was here.

"There is a room on the lower levels that you might like. Whatever you want it to look like is up to you. I'm letting you have the same freedom that I have given Weston, the doctor." He asked her what that meant. "He wanted the state-of-the-art equipment. Before he entered the clinic, there was nothing there. Not even walls. But he said he would work for us if he could have it set up the way he wanted. I don't think he's realized that he set the room up on his own."

"You have that much power?" She looked at Remy when Hector asked her. "Or is it both of you together that makes it? I know that the building was your doing. Right from the moment you started working it, I knew that you were strong. I just had no idea how strong."

"The house is the same way. From the outside, it looks like a large warehouse. But once you enter...well, you'll have to see how much different it is from there." The door opened and Skylar let Hector and the others enter before her. Once they were in the large kitchen, Hector stopped moving and stared at the woman sitting at the table. It was his housekeeper.

"How did you get here?" Mary stood up and sobbed in his arms. She was still crying when she sat back down. "Oh Mary, did he hurt you?"

"No. I'm too old for him to pull the wool over my eyes. But I lied to him. Told him that your son had passed in the night. I knew he'd be back, you see. I just was ready for him. Had a child that had passed a day ago. I hated to do it, I surely did, but I had to save one if I could. And little Ruben didn't harm no one. So when he asked me what I'd done with him, I showed him the paper saying that I'd turned him over to be cremated. The boy that died, he would have been in a poor grave all alone." She looked at Ann. "She brought me here. I was planning a visit anyway and knew that if that man ever found out, I'd be next. He said that he'd take care to get me home safely and while he was out...well, I called me in a favor and had someone bring me here. Ann said I could help out with the house. If the missus don't mind."

"I don't." Skylar smiled at the two women. They were sisters, she'd bet real money on it. They had the same stout built and the no nonsense kind of look in their faces. And Ann looked so happy to see her that there was no way she'd make her leave. "I think Ann was saying she was going to need some help anyway, and this is perfect."

As they made their way to the lower levels, she had a sudden thought. If Dolin were to come here, would he be able to cross over too? Christ that would be just fucking great. Protecting them like this would be nothing compared to the magic that he might have. Skylar decided to talk to Remy about it later. As Weston took them to see Ruben, she went to see the young wolf, Jarvis.

He was watching television when she knocked and turned it off as soon as she came in. Sitting up higher in the bed, she could see that he was looking much better than he had a few days ago. She asked him about it.

"I wasn't able to shift right away but now that I have, things are working their way out of my system. I saw him. The monster that he is. He flew down to the earth and stalked us. I've been hurt before, but that man…he did things to me." She nodded. Remy had spoken to Jarvis just yesterday and had told her what had happened. But he hadn't mentioned that Jarvis saw the creature. "He pulled me into his thrall and I was hooked."

"Remy said that he tried something sexual on you." Jarvis flushed and nodded. "You don't have to tell me too. But I would like to know what you saw. It would go a long way into helping us."

"I didn't remember until today what he was. I think that my mind needed to cope with this before it could what I'd seen." He pulled back the sheet that covered him, and Skylar looked at the scar. "He blasted me with something powerful. At first I thought it was a flame thrower but as soon as I got to cover, I knew it was magic. It even smelled like it."

The gash was perhaps twenty-four inches long. It was wide and puckered in places where it had been stitched together. Weston said it was the only way to keep the boy from bleeding out until he was well enough to shift. There were other wounds too, not as large but just as nasty. She wondered, not for the first time, how he'd ever gotten to them. But having Catherine here and their ability to communicate with each other had been all he'd needed.

Weston said that he'd have to pledge to an alpha before the scar would go away. She didn't understand that, of course, but Weston assured her that he'd be fine. But the nightmares worried him a great deal. She asked Jarvis again what he'd seen.

"At first I thought it was a large hawk. I've seen a few of them around, but this seemed to get bigger the closer he got. His one wing was as wide as my truck, and there were two of them. Claws were at his hands and feet. Like really big, sharp ones. You ever see that movie that had the alien that got on the ship in space?" She nodded. "He looked like her in the face. Not the actress, but the monster. His mouth was huge and full of the sharpest teeth you've ever seen. But when he came closer to us on the ground, he was just normal. Well, sort of normal."

"We have caught him." Jarvis seemed to curl into himself. "He's not here. But we have him chained up. The men he bit, they're dead. But you survived. Do you have any idea why he didn't bite you?"

"I think he realized almost too late what I was." She asked him what he meant. "That thing…he's not a person but a thing. He pulled my head back and nearly bit me like the others. But he had to smell what I was. When I hit him, knocking him away from us, I could see that he was confused. But finally he started to take off again. I got a good bite into his leg, but it cost me. His blood filled my mouth, and that's what made me sick I think."

"It was." He nodded and leaned back against the pillow. "And Catherine, she told you where to come?"

"No. Not really. I knew where she was because she told me, but I didn't tell her I was hurt. I didn't want the baby to be hurt by her worrying." She nodded. "It's not mine. The baby. It's not mine. But she is my mate."

"I don't understand a great deal about your kind." He nodded. "Will you...do you plan to raise it up as your own? I mean, I sort of know that your kind is very possessive."

"Yes. He's her child and I love her. We've been waiting to convert her until she has the baby but now that she's safe, I don't have to worry so much. Her dad, he's a piece of shit." Skylar nodded. "Did she tell you that he tried to get her to give him information on races? And when she explained to him that she couldn't, he beat her?"

"I've only spoken a little with her. She's very shy." He grinned, and Skylar had a feeling that she wasn't shy around him. "Who does the baby belong to? Her father?"

"No. His best friend." He didn't tell her anything more, but she got it. Her father had more than likely let the man have his granddaughter in return for something. When he nodded, as if he knew what she was thinking, Skylar stood up. "I'll leave after the babe is born. We'll need to find us a safe place to live, but I'll come back for them."

"You'll stay here with us." He started to protest. "You heard me. We need men like you here. You're going to be very helpful in our fight against these things. And Catherine will have her mom."

As she left the younger man to his rest, she thought about what was going on. All the changes of her life in the last month. And the amount of people that she and Remy were protecting. Grabbing the wall beside her, she stood there for several seconds just holding on. That was when Remy came up behind her and wrapped his arms around her.

"Overwhelmed?" She nodded. "Yeah, me too. There a great many people here and we're responsible for them all against an untold amount of monsters on the outside that simply want to kill us all and take over the world."

She turned in his arms. "You are so not helping me right now. I just told Jarvis that he was staying here too. I'm not sure what he can do to help us, but there you have it. And the lab that we took over this last night is now ours. The paperwork came via carrier this morning. The name it came under was a little off. What did you do?"

"Nothing. I swear." He took her hand to his mouth and kissed her palm. "When this is all over, if it's ever over, will you marry me?"

"Seriously?" He nodded. "What for? I mean we're happy this way, right? And how the hell would we explain your birth certificate. Do you even have one?"

"I have been around for a long time and have needed it over the years. There are those that would help a man in my position." She stared at him, wondering for a moment what it would be like to live for so flipping long. He kissed her nose. "Do not think on things that you cannot fix, love. You will only make yourself crazy."

"I am crazy." He nodded, and she slapped him. "I love you. I don't think I say that enough to you."

"I shall make it my hourly priority to say it to you more often as well. I love you as well." He pulled her body to his. "I love what you do to me when we're alone. I love the way you scream out my name when you come. You have no idea how—"

The throat clearing behind them had them both turning. Jake was standing there grinning for several seconds before his face turned serious again.

"We have some movement. Toward the lab. Oh, and you might receive a letter in the mail about the building. I did a little working around, and you both now own it.

Well, your new company does." She asked him what company as they followed him into the command center. Jarvis was at one of the computers working, and Jake just shook his head. "I looked him up, Rembrandt the artist. His name was Rembrandt Harmenzoon van Rijn. Any relationship?"

Skylar looked at Remy, but he didn't answer. She looked back at Jake. "Is this legal? I mean, is this going to come back and bite us in the ass later?"

"No. You do have to make arrangements to pay the taxes after the fifty-year abatement you got. The renovations, my idea by the way, should start when you get a crew lined up. Some of your fancy improvements to it every once in a while should keep even the most nosey mayor out of the thing. And the work that Weston is doing there is going to be a lot of help for a great many people."

As they looked over his shoulder at the computer screen, Skylar once again had the overwhelming urge to run and hide from this all. But she looked over at Jarvis and saw that he was running several programs at once. Two of them seemed to be tracking the monsters. The other she had no idea. He looked at her.

"I'm sort of a nerd." Nodding, she looked at his screens more closely. "That guy that attacked me, I got his name from Weston. He's a wolf too. But he gave me his name, and I've been looking for any accounts he has. It might not be nothing, but then again, we're going to need money to run this operation."

Nodding, she looked back at the other screen. Christ, she thought, I'm so in over my head. And the water was getting deeper all the time.

Chapter 12

Davis was right behind him as he and Skylar moved out of the large SUV that seemed to have come with the garage. Things were running to the very weird at the house and while most of it he understood the need for, some things, like the added rooms, he did not.

There were now nearly twenty bedrooms in the house. He'd asked Skylar about it, but she'd told him other than the twelve that they were told they'd need and the ones for Ann and Mary, she didn't know. He had a feeling that they both knew more than they thought they did.

The building was quiet. Weston had told them that he was in the top two floors, going back and forth between the lab part of the building and down to the rooms where Benton was being held. He'd told them that the man was making enough noise to wake the dead, and Remy said he'd look into it.

The few malefactors that were milling around looked more confused than angry. As they walked up to them, they parted like they were not sure what do to about them either. Skylar looked inside the door, then came out.

"They got in." He nodded, figuring that something would break this place sooner or later. "I mean, there are a lot of them in there. All of them looking like these guys. What's going on, do you suppose?"

"Maybe they're here to rescue Benton but just don't know how to do it." Davis moved closer to one of the faded guys, and he too walked away. "This is just weird. Do you suppose we can go by them inside? I mean, maybe they're up there waiting for Weston to come out of the room?"

The elevators weren't working yet. But they did take the stairs. It was only five flights and they made short work of that. But the floor where Weston was working was empty of them. In fact, there wasn't a sound to be heard at all.

"Something is wrong." Remy agreed with Skylar. "Where is the shouting he said was going on? And for that matter, where is Weston? Wasn't he supposed to wait on us?"

"Yes. Let's split up and go see what we can find. I'll go up; Davis, you go down; and Skylar, you stay here. I don't know what we might find so if you hear anything, go to that person." He wanted to tell her to run, but he knew that the only way she'd run was in the direction of trouble. So to save himself from being mad when she did it, he told her to. "Just be careful and make sure that you kill first instead of later."

Remy kissed her on the mouth quickly and left them. Taking the stairs two at a time, he found himself on the fifth floor in seconds. As soon as he opened the door, he knew that he was going to get hurt.

Weston looked like he'd been beaten to shit. Several times, then ran over. Benton, in what Remy could only assume was his true form, was holding him up by his neck. The monster's tongue came out and burned a long gash into Weston's chest.

"Mine." He took a step toward him and said it again, his clawed feet digging deep into the floor. "You will leave me to my work, Rembrandt. This creature is all mine for what he has done to me."

"You were imprisoned. How did you get out?" The thing laughed, and Remy put his hand on his hip. He had no idea if the gun would hurt the thing or piss it off more, but he had to try. "And you're not going to get out of here alive. I do hope you know that."

"I have not lived for this long and not have all kinds of ways to escape, Rembrandt. Or do I call you Remy?" The creature moved toward him again, his wings were spread out now and they dug into the walls as he moved. "Would you trade yourself for him? I do believe you'd go down better than a wolf."

"No. Please don't do it." Remy didn't bother looking at Weston when he spoke. He was keeping an eye on Benton. "He's going to kill us both."

"No he's not." Weston was thrown at him and Remy just barely got out of the way. The sickening crush of bones sounding behind him had Remy wanting to go to the other man, but he knew that he couldn't, not and save them both. When the threat of a hostage was gone, Remy pulled his gun.

"You think that thing is going to save you?" The laughter made his skin crawl; his blood seemed to curdle in his veins. But it was loud and Remy hoped that Skylar or Davis heard him. "I have long since perfected my body to fight against such things as that. I am the perfect killing machine. I can kill and not be killed. You will see."

"Yet we captured you." The snarl and the lash of his tongue at him had Remy backing up. The cut of the hot slice to his chest made him think that all of his belly was spilling out, but there was nothing to show that he'd been cut other than the tear in his shirt and the blood on it. "Is that all you have?"

He'd heard it in a movie some time ago. When he'd been fascinated by the moving art on the screen. He'd go to the theater and sit for hours watching the moving pictures as they filled the large screen. Remy knew now that the things that he'd seen there, the monsters that were make believe, were nothing compared to this thing.

The closer he got to him, the more he could see. The fact that he was still being held up on this floor astounded him. He was bigger than anything he'd ever seen.

The scales on his body seemed to fade from the royal blue that he was in human form to the palest of blues of the soldiers. He wondered then if the man had more to do with their creation than they'd thought. When Benton put out his hand, as if in greeting, Remy took another step back.

"You should never have come here." Benton laughed at him. "You're going to die, you know. You and Dolin. And once you're all dead, we're going to never think on you again."

"You think now, my dear Rembrandt? I'm surprised at you. Do you not think of your children all the time? And that lovely wife of yours? Is she so faded from your mind that you do not remember her apple pie? I do. I remember a great deal about your pretty family."

He saw Skylar and Davis, but his mind was too busy to register that they were talking to him. His wife? How had this thing known his wife? As he stared at the thing, he realized two things at once. Remy was going to die and that Skylar was going to be pissed.

The claw came at him. And on some level, Remy knew that he should move, but there wasn't enough time. It touched his chest, dug deep into him, and he stood there. It wasn't until the thing pulled away, letting him drop to the floor, that Remy realized that he'd been lifted up. His body hit the floor so hard that he felt it give under his weight.

The winged creature was fighting for all it was worth. Remy tried to stand up, but his legs didn't seem to want to support him. Looking down at them, he saw that they were shattered and bones were sticking out of his flesh at odd angles. The monster screamed at him, looking up. Davis was helping him move.

"She's going to fucking kill it." He looked at the monster and was about to tell Davis it was a man from his past when he realized that it was Skylar. She was fighting the monster and winning too. "Get up. Damn it all to fuck. I can't lift you without your help."

The other side of his body was lifted up. Remy stared at Weston as he helped Davis carry him. The man wasn't dead, his befuddled mind told him, and he smiled at Weston. Remy was hurting in so many places that when he'd asked him where it hurt, Remy replied that it was everywhere. He looked at the creature and Skylar once again.

The guns in her hands were doing more damage than he'd thought they'd do. He pulled his own free of his hips and aimed them both at the thing's belly. Remy wasn't sure if the bullets would hurt or not, but the gun in his mouth was doing some major damage. Skylar was using them both like a spoon, filling him with lead.

The gun in his hand fired. He supposed he'd meant to, but the bullets dug deep into the monster's belly. As it screamed, it tossed Skylar away from him and she hit the wall. Remy tried to crawl to her, but all he managed to do was move only a few inches. The ceiling above him exploded in light, and he looked up just as it rained down on top of them.

Remy watched as Benton flew away out the opening he'd made. The sky was dark one second, lighter the next. Each time he moved his blackened wings, he would blot out the sun. Remy lay there. His entire body hurt beyond anything he'd ever felt, and he remembered Skylar. Turning, he cried out. She was broken, was all he could think of.

~~~

Hector had just read his son a story, the fifth one in the hour that he'd been with him, when he heard something. He wasn't sure what it was but stood up with his child behind him. Ruben had long since fallen asleep, only waking when the book was finished to ask for another. This time he didn't stir as the noises beyond his room grew louder.

When nothing broke into the room he was in, he cautiously moved to the door. There was no way he was going to give his son's position away so he peaked around the door at the hall. When he realized what he was seeing was true, he opened the door wider and moved down the hall with the fast moving gurneys. Someone was seriously hurt.

It took him several seconds to realize that the bloodied mess on the bed was Skylar. And a few minutes more to see that there was a second bed that held Rembrandt. There was little he could do for them so was shoved out of the way by the crew working there. The nine people around Skylar looked grim.

"She's going to make it." Hector looked at Davis. "Never in my life would I have thought she could have taken that thing on and come out on top like she did."

Hector looked at the woman on the bed. If she had come out on top, he was terrified to see what was on the bottom. She was dead; her heart had just not given up as yet. He looked at the man who was on the other bed.

Rembrandt had not fared much better. But he looked as if he'd been beaten to near death rather than brutalized as Skylar did. His legs were wrapped in a sheet that was covered in blood. His face looked as if parts of it were broken beneath the flesh and lay sagging against the bone. There were marks on his chest that Hector had seen before. Marks of a tongue, hot and sharp, that had been lay against human flesh. But neither of them were human.

"Dad?" He looked at his son, who had wandered into the room. Before he could pick him up and get him to cover, he spoke again. "They have wings. They have to hide."

He picked his son up in his arms, trying his best to shield him from the bodies on the beds. The couple had worked so hard and now it was over for them. But Ruben struggled again. Insisting that they needed to hide.

"Hide where? Where do you think they can go?" Weston was covered in blood. His lab coat looked as if he'd been bathing it the red mire. But he looked at Ruben as if he held all the answers. "What do you think we should try?"

"They need to...I can't remember what it's called." Reuben pulled from him, and he set him down. He ran out of the room so quickly that Hector was both proud to see him moving and terrified he'd get hurt. But when he returned with a book in his hand, he gave it to Weston. "Daddy was reading this. That's what they have to do."

He'd been reading a story about cocoons and how the caterpillar would make one and crawl into it to change. He had no idea where the book had come from, but he'd read it when Reuben had asked him to. Weston looked at the pages, then at him.

"Can you draw out their wings? I'm assuming they have them." Hector said he had no idea, but they could look. Rolling over, Remy caused him to scream, but they saw the tats there. "Can you do it? You're their maker of sorts. Can you wrap them in their wings?"

Hector had no idea. These people were nothing like he'd thought. They were more than him. Hell, they were more than anything he'd ever encountered before. But he walked to Remy and put his hand on his head.

The connection was light. He thought it was because the man was so near dying. Or as he found out from looking into his brain, giving up. He knew that his mate was nearly dead and he didn't want to go on without her. So Hector dug deeper until he found the place where he'd stretched out his wings and moved into the thought.

"Rembrandt, you—" A hand touched his arm. Davis. He said that his name was Remy. That might work better. Nodding, he went back to his task. "Remy, I need for your wings to come out. Pull them. Pull them or you will die."

"She will die." He looked at Weston. "Not him, her. She will die if he can't figure this out. I think…I have no idea but if you can pull his, she'll be able to pull hers. Or he will. Fuck, I have no idea. I've never had a patient that had wings, much less as much power as these two do. Pull them for her."

"Remy, Skylar will die if you do not wake the fuck up and wrap her." The mind stirred a little against him. Hector felt encouraged and tried again. "Do you want her to die? Do you want all that she's done to be for nothing? If not, then wake your hiney up and get her well."

"Hiney?" He looked at his son, then at Weston. "I'm pretty sure that you using the word 'fuck' a few times is a hell of a lot worse than 'ass.' Just making an observation here."

Before he could say anything, Remy sat up. His body was ramrod straight and his eyes were hardly focused. But the wings that spread behind him were full and in amazing shape. He looked at him for several seconds, then at Skylar. She stirred but didn't move.

"Skylar. Come to me." She stirred yet again, but nothing more. Remy looked at them all. "Bring her to me. Put her on me."

The gurney moved to the other bed almost on its own. Weston told each of them to take a corner and not to let go until she was safe. As soon as they picked her up, the scream almost made Hector drop her again but they got her to Remy. He pulled her body to him and lay back down. His wings were wrapping around him even as he closed his eyes.

Each of them stood there. Hector wanted to see what was going on within those dark wings but was afraid of disturbing whatever he was doing to heal them both. The bed was moved to another room and the door shut behind them as Weston entered with them. Hector looked at Davis when he started picking up the bloodied towels around the room.

"She leapt up on that monster like she knew just what she was doing. He kept hitting her with his tongue, tearing at her skin, but she never gave up. Protecting what was hers, I'm guessing. Remy was already beat up pretty bad by the time we got up there to him." Hector started picking up some of the mess as well and tried to imagine his wife trying to save him. She would, she did on several occasions when he'd been hurt in battle. "I tried to help them. She told me to get to Weston and Remy and to get them out of the building. But he was too beat up and I could hardly get him to stand up. Then that wolf of Weston's came out of nowhere and he helped me. But it was nearly too late for them. The monster threw her at the wall twice with his claws in her chest before Remy shot him in the chest."

"Did they kill it?" Davis shook his head. "Where is he? Do you know? Tell me what he looked like and maybe we can track him."

"The devil himself. And Remy was able to shoot him in the chest with one of those guns on his hip. The scale, the thing had scales, but Skylar had managed to get a few of them off him. The way she was tearing into him, I'm wondering why he didn't lose them all. But she got a couple off and that's where he was shot. In the bare place."

"Was it Benton?" Davis nodded and turned to look at him. The room was clean. There was nothing else he could do to avoid the truth. He knew what the thing was. "He was made not by us in our world but by his own hand. I didn't find him, find out about him until later. I don't know what he is."

"He said some things to Remy just before Skylar attacked him. I'm not sure what it meant, but it was something to do with some pie. Does that mean anything to you?" Hector shook his head. "Me neither, but whatever it was sure did shock the shit out of Remy."

Hector waited for Weston to come out of the room. He'd changed into something a little cleaner, but he was still covered in blood. When Hector asked if he could sit with the couple, he told him he could but not to touch them. He agreed that he wouldn't and went into the dark room and sat down.

"I know you probably can't hear me, but I wanted to tell you how sorry I am. I know that you wished to die that day. You were so close to it that I changed you before you were ready. But you've come so far now. And with Skylar there, I'm thinking that you might just beat this thing." He reached for the book on the smallish table and opened it up. He grinned at the cover. It was one of the kinds of books his wife favored.

She had read like it was her duty. The light to their bedroom on until all hours when she'd tell him just one more chapter. The books, she'd told him, were to give her peace of mind. He would come to this realm just to get her some by the bags full. He wondered what he would do with them now. Laying the book back for something a little less sexual, he found a book about a whale, one he'd read several times himself.

As he opened the first page of the book, he looked at the cocoon on the bed. There was no doubt that Rembrandt could heal himself, but the girl... Hector shook his head. He'd seen worse on the battlefield and those men were long gone. But she had spirit and she loved the big warrior. Hopefully it would be enough.

Instead of reading to them, as was his plan, he thought about Benton. It had been a month or so after the day he'd found Rembrandt…Remy. He'd come upon him while he'd been shadowed and watching some children play in the park near his home. It had been a long time before the illness had closed down that park and a great many more. The children were too ill or were dying by the hundreds now.

"I should like to fight with you. I have spoken to Master Dolin and he said that it would be fine with him if it is for you." The man smiled at him, and Hector had taken a step back. "You shouldn't be afraid of me. I'm harmless."

"I'm not afraid of you." He was, though, and he was sure the man knew it. "I don't care if you fight in the wars. But you are to only kill what needs to be killed. We're not in this for mass murders." Benton had smiled at him again and there were fangs there. "What are you?"

"Me? I am nothing more than one of your soldiers. But I will be more someday soon." He looked at the children before continuing. "So many will die. They will not even know what harmed them."

"The children?" Benton looked at him then and assured him he meant the enemy. But even to this day, Hector had not believed him. But when the people, his friends and their friends, started to die with some illness, it was all he could think about in those first few days that Benton had had something to do with it.

"I fear that he had more to do with everything than any of us could have imagined." The dark cocoon stirred, but no sound came from it. He picked up the book again and began reading. He so loved this book.

"Chapter one. Call me…"

Chapter 13

Dolin was looking everywhere he could think of. How could a man disappear so completely? And he couldn't get in touch with Benton either. Dolin sat down on the couch that he'd given Hector so long ago. Where the hell was the man?

"I have been to the other realm." He looked up at Ward. "He's not anywhere near the compound, and if he's inside of it, I can't tell that either. What the hell did you say to him?"

"Nothing. I gave him the glass of poison and sent him off to bed. He'd drunk half of it before I even left. By now he should be in pain, not gone out somewhere." Dolin got up to go to the bedroom again. The glass, he just realized, was missing too. It was one of the reasons he'd come back today. First to find out how close to death Hector was and to collect his glass. He'd been so careful so far to make sure that he never left evidence around.

"The glass is gone too. So wherever he is, he's not in the other realm with it. Nothing transports that way. I made sure of it." He'd worked hard on it. The first few times he'd ended up naked in the other realms. It had taken him nearly a decade to perfect it. "Perhaps he's staying with that woman of his. The maid or whatever she was. I haven't been to her house yet, but I'm betting he's there. She's more than likely taking care of him like she did the wife and brat."

"I'll send someone over there." Ward left the room and Dolin looked around. The room smelled of the two of them. He'd never really cared for Margo anyway, and when she'd taken her last breath, he'd been, there to see it. The bitch had been a thorn in his side for a long time. But the room was off. He'd never really looked around much when he'd been here, but there was very definitely something off about it. He walked to the bathroom and kicked a box of woman's product across the room. He picked it up and looked inside.

He could see that something had spilled in the box. But whatever it had been was now absorbed into the long tubes. He tried tearing the one that looked to be the most saturated, but it yielded nothing more than more fiber. Dolin threw the entire box in the trash can.

"There's nobody there. The whole house they said looks like it's been ransacked." Dolin started to ask him what was off about the room when he looked at the trashcan. "What the fuck are you doing?"

Christ, he knew then. "He put the glass in here. He was trying to hide it. I don't know from who or why, but he did."

"So?" He looked at Ward. He was one of the smartest men he knew. For years Dolin had looked up to him in so many things. But right now he would have gladly slapped the shit out of him. "What do you care if he hid the glass or not?"

"He knew what was in it." Ward stared at him for several seconds. Then it was as if a light went off and he could suddenly see. "Yeah. If he knew then he had reason to run. And he didn't drink anything. The tricky bastard."

Dolin was somewhat impressed. Hector was still going to die, but the fucker was smart enough not to trust him. That meant that he'd be a little harder to get close to. No matter, he'd just let Rembrandt deal with him. Ward was grinning when he started to ask him what would be a good reason to have him killed.

"You do know that if he knows you're in on this, he's not going to trust you ever again." Dolin was thinking the man had lost his mind. He was ready to tell him he had it, that he'd take care of everything so as not to get them caught, but he continued before he could. "But...he doesn't know I'm a part of it. For all he knows, you and I are enemies. That little trick you pulled last year with his wife solidified that deal."

He'd made a pass at Margo and she'd slapped him. Ward had come to her rescue when he'd been about to hit her. With a wink at him, Ward had cursed him and told him to leave. Margo had been running to Ward whenever Hector was out since. Even going to him when she'd thought that Dolin had been poisoning her. It was what had accelerated her death. Her death meant she couldn't blab to Hector and ruin all their plans.

Their plans. And oh what plans they were. Take over the earth and make it just the way they wanted it. Riches everywhere. The stupid people had no idea what sort of treasures they had at their fingertips that would make them rich beyond anything they could imagine. And Dolin had imagined a great deal.

There were currently twelve other realms that used the agate that was lying about in that world. It had properties in it that was used in all sorts of magic. One realm used it to clean and purify their air and water. They were going to be his best customers.

Humans used it in jewelry if it suited them but for the most part, they ignored it. Day after day they'd walk by the small stones that he'd give everything for. And he had. The orders coming in for them were amazing. And very profitable. Just as soon as the humans were gone.

"We should send more of the soldiers to that realm. Soon. I'd like to just get this over with, and the sooner the better as far as I'm concerned." Dolin nodded at Ward but said nothing. Too soon, he thought, but let Ward talk. "How long will it take to make about two thousand more of them?"

"A few weeks. The things we have going on here is making it hard to get volunteers. Especially when we are at peace." That had been a major mistake on his part. Peace meant no money for the labs to run the men and women through. Had a war raged, the people of this world would have been throwing gold at them. "Not to mention, putting the blood in the water systems that run through the poorer parts of town has made the pickings sort of slim. We'll need to go out and get them if we want anyone to work with us."

"I don't see a problem with that." Of course he didn't. So long as he didn't have to do it. But Dolin didn't have time to fuck around with gathering a fold here. He wanted things to progress on the other realm so he could have the coin. "I'll see if I can make up something that will show them how we're in need again. Perhaps we can make up a little story about something going on in another realm that needs our help."

"You do that." After Ward left him, Dolin looked around the house. There was little here. Pictures that were old, a few things that the brat had made for his parents. The closets were stuffed full of crap, not even a decent suit among the things that Hector had left behind. And he had too. There was no doubt about it.

Hector could have been such a great addition to their team. From the first, he'd been helpful in all their tests, DNA testing and all the other things he'd done aside, he had a great head on his shoulders for the working part of their plan. But he'd gotten stupid. And by stupid Dolin meant he'd had morals. He remembered talking to him about it several months ago.

"You can make a lot of money by using what you know, and my contacts." Dolin watched as he literally backed away from him. "Come on, Hector. Don't you want a better life for you and your family?"

"I have a good life with them now. We don't owe anyone. Our home is just the way we like it. Rueben is in the best schools we could find. Life for us is just the way we want it. More money? No thanks. Not at the risk of having something made by me becoming a monster." Dolin had laughed to himself even then. He'd already created a monster. He just didn't know it. "I like things the way they are."

"Ward and I are going to branch out. We were hoping that you could come with us." Again and again he'd told him no, he was fine. "I'm not sure what to say to you that'll change your mind. Help me here."

"There will be nothing to change my mind about. I've already talked to Margo about this. I figured that you'd not be satisfied with the way things were going and we've decided to stay where we are. Happily." Dolin tried again, but Hector had simply walked away. And now...now he was out there somewhere with the knowledge to make them richer than they were already going to be.

Dolin actually considered destroying the home. He really hated this place. It was so...he supposed it was so like Hector and Margo. Soft like she was; dull like he was. The only bright spot had been the kid. He was a sharp one too.

Standing out on the little porch, he looked out over the dismal view. "Where are you, Hector? Hiding in a cave somewhere? Or have you gone to one of your few friends? You're not with your buddy Rembrandt. The man hates you. So where could you be?"

~~~

Davis sat in the kitchen. He supposed he should eat the meal that was in front of him, but all he could think about was the couple downstairs. If they died...well, Hector assured him that they wouldn't die, not now, but if something happened to them that they no longer could fight, he had no idea what to do with himself.

"You need to eat." Ann shoved the plate closer to him. "You think they're gonna come on up out of that thing and not kick some ass? They're gonna be stronger for this."

"How do you know?" She didn't say anything but sat down across from him with a cup of tea. "Ann, I know that I've not been here long, none of us have, but damn it, I love them. They're the best thing that has happened to me in all my life."

"Me too. And my granddaughter too. Did you know that they're giving her care like it was their job? Hired in a doc just to be here in the event she needs something. That swelling that was in her knees?" Davis nodded. "She was not resting enough. He told her to sit for four or five hours a day with her feet up. Cured it right now. I tried to tell her to rest, but I'm just her mom. I don't know any better."

"You must be getting excited about the baby." Her grin told him she was more than excited. "How many pairs of booties have you knitted for him?"

"Two...well, two dozen, but that's not bad. I have five blankets I made too. And you know what? With this job and that man of mine not taking it all for drinking, I'm able to go online and buy her things too. Stuff we didn't get to take with us when we left home." He'd heard that there was sort of a blow up when she'd left but not any details other than what had been rumored. "What did you leave behind?"

"Nothing. And I'm not kidding either. I had a job that I had to leave when the cancer started to slow me down. An apartment that sucked. I didn't even have a table and chairs to sit on. No friends other than a few on the job. And my family is all gone. I didn't even have a dog or cat. Just me." He thought of the day he'd been in the hospital. "I was laying there all hooked up to every machine there was when this man walks in. Hector, of course, but I didn't know that then. He was dressed from head to toe in black, and I thought he was the grim reaper coming to get me. Welcomed it actually. I hurt that bad."

Ann got up and poured them some more tea. His plate was empty. He'd not even realized that he'd eaten anything, so she took that as well. When she sat back down, she nodded at him to continue.

"He asked me if I wanted to work with him. I told him I was in no shape to piss by myself, so I think not." He flushed slightly and told her he was sorry for being so crude. "I worked with hard men and harder criminals. I should know better around a pretty lady like you."

"Oh go on with you. I'm old enough to be your mother." She slapped his hand. "Go on. Tell me what brought you here."

"He told me that my body would need some adjustments, and that was the least of his worries. He then asked me if I would work with a man so great that it would make me want to pray to him. That the woman with him would be my confidant. That I would no longer hurt or need the gun that I'd given up."

But he did hurt at times. He supposed that was a good thing. To be painless would be…he supposed it would be worse than feeling it all. Davis looked at Ann and smiled.

"I'm older than I look. Here, let me show you something." He pulled out his driver's license, the only thing besides his wallet that he had taken that day. Davis showed it to her. "I'm nearly forty. I know that I look younger. Hell, I look like I'm in my mid-twenties and I have to tell you, I never looked this good in my twenties."

"And you got this because you came to work with Mr. Remy?" Davis nodded. There was more, of course. A great deal more he'd gotten from the man, but most of it he was still trying to deal with. Like the biting thing. He still had a little trouble with that. "You have tattoos too, like Mr. Remy and Miss Skylar?"

"I do." He lifted up his shirt and showed her what he had. "There are guns too. I just have them when I need them. And there is a sword at my back that peels away."

Davis stood up and showed her. He was terrified of cutting himself every time he pulled it from his back, but so far he'd been lucky. And it had come in really handy when the shit hit the fan at the hospital.

"What happened?" He looked at Ann and wondered how she knew. Then he remembered that she was a telepath. "They can't tell me and you have been so sad. Tell me what happened and maybe...I don't know, maybe you'll feel better."

"He was so...monstrous. I don't mean just big, and he was fucking huge. His legs were as big as I was; his claws were as long as my arm. As soon as we come through the door, I knew we were dead. But Skylar? She just jumped onto his back and started stabbing him with her own blades. Christ, you should have seen her. Like some sort of avenging angel come down from the heavens to save us all." He closed his eyes for a second to remember her there before continuing. "I didn't see Remy until she was already fighting the thing. I woke up that doc first. Remy is a tad on the huge side himself."

"He is at that. And Weston said you saved his life too. Had he not shifted when he had, he would have bled out." Davis just nodded. The man was awake, but just a little on the stupor side that was all. "You should have more pride in what you did, Davis. You saved both those men and they know it."

Nodding, he said nothing. "That thing that was there. I'm still trying to figure out what happened. I mean those malefactors seemed to be slow. Like they were on something. And, Christ, was he strong. When he tossed her off him, I thought for sure she was going to go through the wall. And he seemed to get stronger the more he fought."

"Perhaps he was feeding off them somehow." She got up to refresh their tea again, and it suddenly hit him. She was right. That's what it was doing. Why it had gathered them there. When Ann turned back to him, she looked concerned. Before she could say another word, he picked her up and hugged her tightly.

"You should be in the command center. And if I didn't enjoy every meal that you make me, I'd take you there myself. You're so right." She asked him about what. "He's feeding from them. Somehow he's feeding from them, draining them so he can be stronger. And wherever he's hiding right now, you can bet there are hundreds of those things close by to help him heal.

Davis ran down the stairs two at a time. His mind was buzzing with details. Every time Benton was around, there were malefactors. And most of the time, they were sort of stupid. More so than they were when he wasn't around. He tried to think what they had used to imprison him, but all his mind was focused on was he'd been feeding from them.

"There's no change before you ask." He sat down at the table that Weston was working at. "I've just checked on them. And other than the fact that I can hear two hearts beating, that's it. No change."

"They need more of us around them." Weston looked at him. "That monster, what do you remember about him?"

"That he lured me into the room by compulsion and that once I was there, he made me unlock the cage. I have no idea how he'd done that. I'm usually very strong when it comes to fighting it off." He looked up from the charts he was working on. "Why do you ask?"

"Were there any malefactors there when you were working? Or sometime during the time he lured you in?"

Weston leaned back in his seat as if he were contemplating his answer. "It's really important that you tell me."

"Okay. I was working in the floor above him. I'd gone out of the building to get a breath of fresh air. I'm a wolf. I love it out of doors. And I noticed that there were a few milling around. Not a lot, but there seemed to be a few more gathering as I was up there. I never thought anything about it because they weren't supposed to be able to get into the place. I didn't know until this morning it was only the upper floors. That way it wouldn't be suspicious if anyone came around." Davis nodded, smiling. "What are you trying to figure out? Because I'd very much like to help you. Before I beat myself up over what I should have done."

"They were feeding him. I think. Well, it wasn't my idea but Ann's. I was telling her how much stronger he was then I'd ever seen and that there were lots of malefactors there. She said perhaps he was feeding from them. And I think she's right." Weston was nodding, and Davis was feeling better about this theory. "What if, and I mean this is a big what if, but what if he was only able to lure you in there because of all the malefactors? For days before he'd not been able to. So what changed then?"

"He called them there. I mean just a few at first, like I saw then as he fed off them to get stronger, more came." Weston stood up and started to pace. "So you're thinking that Remy and Skylar might be able to feed from us. That we'd make them stronger by just being there and letting them take what they need energy-wise."

"It's worth a try." He looked around the spacious room. "How many people do you have working here now?"

"A dozen here and at least that many at the lab. Clean up. I don't know where they're coming from but some show up all the time. They want to help." Davis had noticed that as well. There was a huge staff of people working here too above grounds. Most of them were staying in the little houses that seemed to pop up overnight. A few of them stayed within the building. He'd bet that there were five or six people just working in the yard on clean-up. "Not Catherine. She's doing well enough keeping herself full of energy."

"Okay. How do you suppose we do this?" Weston paced some more. Davis waited. He was a man that thought it out before speaking. Davis was a more of an off-the-cuff sort of guy. He'd throw out idea after idea until one suited him. Whatever worked was how it would work.

"In shifts. We can't just all go in there at once. What if something happens? Then everyone would be drained. No, shifts. I'd say...I'd say we work up slowly. About three or four. If it doesn't work, then we go with more. How many would you say was there with the monster?" Davis thought maybe a hundred and said so. "We don't have that many here. Yet. But we can help them by keeping ourselves rested and eating well. We'll need to tell Ann. She'll have to feed us more than before. And liquids. We'll need to keep hydrated too."

They had a plan. Not a great one, not even what he thought as a good one, but if it worked, it was a fucking fantastic one as far as he was concerned. And Weston told him, several times as they made up the schedule, that no more than an hour at a time. He didn't want anyone sick from this. Davis only wanted them both healthy and awake.

Chapter 14

Remy felt…well, fantastic. He started to stretch out and realized that Skylar was over him. Not wanting to wake her just yet, he tried to think what had happened. Because, as surely as he was lying there, something had.

"You nearly died." Remy looked over at Ann, who was knitting. She continued her task as she spoke. "Scared the lot of them too. Whatever were you thinking getting yourself hurt like that?"

"I'm not sure if I was thinking." He moved his head and looked down at Skylar. "Is she hurt badly?"

"Not any more than you are." He didn't feel hurt, but that didn't mean he wasn't. "Do you remember anything as yet?"

"I was at the clinic and this big ugly thing tried to pull my heart out." She looked up at him. "I'm sorry. I assumed you knew."

"No. We only know what happened from Davis and Weston. What happened prior to that, we're in the dark. But she saved your butt." He nodded, knowing that on some level that they all had. "The doctor is resting, but I'm to wake him as soon as you opened your eyes. I think he was beginning to think the two of you were going to be out for a few more days."

"How long have we been out?" Remy needed to stretch. His wings, they needed to be free as well. As he was trying to think how to do that, Skylar lifted her head and looked at him.

She was bruised still. There was a large gash on her cheek, and her eye was swollen. Surely they couldn't have been here very long if she was still hurt. But when her hand brushed over his cheek, he felt the slight pain.

"Eight days." They both looked at Ann as she stood up, her bag and knitting in her hand. "You were cocooned in your wings for five of those days. Just recently you came out. Then for the last three you've been resting. Just so you know, you look a lot better now than you did when you came out of hiding."

"Cocooned? What do you mean?" But she was going out the door and he was left wondering. Looking at Skylar, he could see that her face was already better and that the swelling was going down. He knew his was as well. Her smile made him feel even better than before.

"You were so hurt." He nodded at her and pulled her up so that he could kiss her. That was when he realized they were naked under the sheet. "I would like a shower. For about three days. And I'm hungry."

"I'm hungry too." He rocked up into her warm flesh. "Very hungry. How about we take a shower together and satisfy both our needs."

She sat up over him and he groaned. Christ, she was beautiful. As she lifted her ass up and lowered herself over him, Remy held his cock. As soon as she was seated, her body tightly wrapped around his in so many ways, he watched her face.

There was something so beautiful about a woman during sex. Especially Skylar when her breasts swayed in rhythm to her movements, her body seemed to hum with energy. Remy loved the way Skylar's mouth tightened when she was close, the way her teeth, her fangs bit deeply into her lower lip. Her nipples were tight and hard and begging to be suckled, but he watched her, holding her tightly to his body.

As she rode him, taking him higher even as she herself was soaring up with him, he couldn't help but love her. Everything about this woman made him realize how lonely he'd been before. Sitting up, he took first one then the other breast to his mouth and bit her, suckling at her blood until she curled her fingers into his hair and pulled him up. Her offer of her throat made his cock harder, his body ready to take as well as give.

"Take me." Remy bit deeply into her neck, the hot, spicy blood filled his mouth as she cried out her release. He took of her greedily, drinking from her even as she came a second then a third time. When he lifted his head, he nearly came. The look on her face, the pure look of lust took his breath away.

Sliding off the bed, he held her on his cock. He needed to fuck her, pound her as hard as he could while she took from him. Fingers dug hard into his back, his wings stretched out and blanketed them in warmth and shelter. As soon as he pressed her to the wall, his cock pistoning into her heat in quick, hard strokes, Remy gave her his own vein and emptied into her when she sank into him.

Holding her while she fed, he fucked her slower now. His cock, emptied for now, seemed to be as greedy for her as his heart was. When she lifted her head from him, holding his gaze with hers, Remy lowered his head to her mouth and kissed her gently, giving her all the love he felt at that moment.

"Something happened to us, didn't it? I mean besides Benton." He didn't bother looking at her as he pulled on his boots. He knew what she meant but wasn't sure what to say. "Remy, are we like him?"

"Christ no." He pulled her into his arms and held her. "Never that. I don't know what's changed but like you, I can feel it. And my wings, they seemed to have…I guess evolved as well."

"That's what it feels like. Like we've evolved." She lifted her head from his chest and looked at him as she continued. "What are we?"

"I don't know. But I intend to find out." They moved up the stairs and went into the kitchen. For some reason it had become the gathering place he'd noticed. Which suited him. Everyone seemed to be there and they looked to be happy to see them.

"Are you hungry?" Ann was the only one that didn't laugh at her question. "There is food for the missus. You are on your own."

"Yes ma'am." Remy sat down and watched the rest of them. There was something going on and no one seemed in a hurry to tell them. Skylar ate her dinner that Ann sat in front of her and they both waited. Someone would start. It just happened to be Rueben.

"You've been resting for a long time, Mr. Remy." The little guy crawled up into his lap and sat facing the table. Remy felt his heart twist just a little when the kid turned and smiled up at him. "Thank you for bringing me my daddy back. I missed him."

"You're very welcome." Remy looked at Davis, then at Weston. "Well? Are you going to make me ask or do you want to spill it?"

"There's more and more being made daily." Weston looked around the room before continuing. "When your wings...when they opened, there was a loud keening noise outside the circle that woke us all up. I guess that was their grieving for you two living. Not that you were going to die, but I think they hoped so. And Davis figured out a few things too."

Remy looked at Davis, who flushed brightly. For a big man, and he was big, he embarrassed easily. Remy wondered if the man had been this way as a human.

"I didn't figure it out. Ann did." The woman popped him in the back of her head with her hand. "Well, you did. She thought maybe Benton was feeding off the malefactor in some way. I just happened to mention it to Weston. He figured out that we need to be near you guys while you recuperated."

"You read to us." Everyone looked at Skylar when she spoke to Hector. "Every time you were in the room, you read to us. I remember thinking that it was amazing how nice your voice was. Do you read to Rueben?"

"I do. It seemed important to me that you knew I was there. Since I'm pretty responsible for putting you in this positon. I'm so sorry for this." The hand to the back of the head nearly had him hit the table. He looked at Ann but said nothing to her. There was a lot of respect there and each of the men knew to give it to her. "Rueben read to you as well."

"I'm getting better too. I can read a whole chapter without missing a single word now." He slid off his lap and kissed his dad. "It's lesson time. I have to go. But I just wanted to tell you I'm glad you're okay."

Remy looked at Hector when his son was gone. "Lesson time? What have we missed in the week and a half we've been out of it?"

"You have no idea." Hector laid a notebook on the table and Weston a file. Remy looked at both of them almost afraid to know what was in them. "After Benton disappeared we put out a full watch on the malefactors. We figure wherever he is, he's going to need some of them to feed from. And Weston had figured out that your heart rate increased when either something funny was read to you or someone was having a jovial conversation. We…Weston and I think that the opposite might be true of Benton. He feeds off the anger."

"That makes sense. I guess. And where is he?" Remy had to work hard at not shivering. The thing…that thing had nearly taken his heart out. He wondered if Hector knew that could happen. And the way he'd tossed Skylar around had… "I need to go outside for a second."

He got up and moved without waiting for an answer. His body needed to be released. It was the only way he could describe what he was feeling. As soon as the sun touched his skin, he nearly cried out in relief. Remy took his shirt off and let his wings free.

"You're not going to like the rest of this." Weston was behind him when he spoke softly. "I'm not even sure that I want to tell you."

"Say it." Weston didn't say anything for several minutes. Remy was all right with that. He was still trying to get his body back. He knew that was a stupid way to think of it, but that's just how it felt. "When we were resting…or whatever it was, something happened to us. Is that what you're afraid to tell me?"

"No. I have no idea what occurred while you two were sleeping. This is more to do with the malefactors than you two." There was silence again before Weston spoke. "They're more of them. Not just…more doesn't even begin to cover it. There are swarms of them. They're hitting towns like a plague, then moving on. Leaving behind the dead, which are in the hundreds. Women and children this time, they're not even caring who they take."

Remy stood up and Weston backed up. Remy had no idea what he was afraid of but when he took another step back, Remy stopped moving.

"I will never harm you." Weston nodded but didn't move. "What is it? Tell me. I'm in bad enough shape right now without you making me feel like I'm about to tear your throat out."

"That's precisely it." Remy frowned. "When I came out here, it was to tell you that there is a problem. But now…have you looked at yourself today? I mean, in the last, oh I don't know, ten minutes?"

Remy looked around. There was no mirror, and he thought perhaps Weston realized what he said when he flushed. Taking a step around the man this time, he made his way to the house. He'd get answers if it was the last thing he did. But as soon as he walked into the kitchen, all thoughts of answers about himself flew out the window.

"Skylar?" She nodded but didn't move. He took a step toward her when she backed up. "What is it? What has happened?"

Her wings were out, and he only just then realized that his were as well. Her face, while still as lovely as ever, was marked with more tats, her neck and arms as well.

And when she put out her hands, he could see that those too, top and bottom, were marked. Hesitantly, he looked at his own.

He was just as marked. Not only his hands, but he had a feeling that his legs too were marred up. Skylar had on a pair of shorts and her legs were tatted up from foot to where the pant leg met her thigh. Everyone turned to the doorway when it darkened. Remy felt his body tense for the worst.

"It's in response to the increase of malefactors. I think...I believe that Mr. Davis will have the same issues." Hector moved more into the room, but slowly. Remy was glad. He had a feeling that he'd hurt him otherwise. "There is more going on, as you are aware. Not with the malefactors, but with you and Miss Skylar. You have evolved."

"Into what?" Skylar took a step toward Hector when he didn't answer right away. "I have this uncontrollable urge to tear you apart. Can you tell me why?"

"I believe it has to do with Dolin. He wishes you to kill me." Remy stood next to Skylar. As soon as he put his hands on her shoulders, he could feel the calmness settle over him. "My son and I will leave soon. It will be much too dangerous for us to remain here. I believe he, Dolin, and Ward have conspired to have me killed."

"You're not leaving." Skylar put out her hand, and that's when Remy saw Rueben. "Come here, please. I won't hurt you."

Ruben walked around his dad and moved to her. When Hector reached out to no doubt bring him back, Skylar growled low. As soon as Reuben touched his hand to hers, Remy felt it.

"We have to keep in contact." Reuben nodded at her as she bent on her knees to talk to him. "You know a great deal more than anyone, I think. What is it?"

"He was giving us some medicine." Skylar nodded but didn't look at Hector when he moaned. "Master Dolin would come by the house when Mary would be gone. He'd give me a glass of stuff, then Mom. I stopped drinking it and put it in the plant."

"You're a very smart young man. I don't suppose you'd let me touch your head, would you? I think I can see just what I need to see from there. I won't hurt you." The little boy nodded and took another step toward her. Skylar looked at Hector before touching him. "I have no idea why I think I can get the information we need like this, but I'd very much like to try."

Hector nodded but said nothing. He was in turmoil, anyone could see that. His son had been hurt, but his friend, his wife was dead because of it. And if not for this son doing something he more than likely felt guilty for, he'd be dead as well.

~~~

Skylar ran her fingers down the little boy's cheek. It was soft and covered in the softest down she'd ever felt. As she looked into his eyes, she put her hand over his head and felt the connection to him sort of punch her in the head. She looked at him once more to see if she had hurt him, but he only winked at her. Cheeky kid. Closing her eyes, she reached into his mind.

"You'll drink all of this down, young man. I know that you do not like the taste, but it will make you better for me." She looked at who she assumed was Dolin from young Rueben's perspective. "Drink it up."

The glass blurred into her vison, then disappeared. When he pulled it to his mouth, Skylar could see that his lips were tight against the glass and that he was thinking where he could dump it. Reuben didn't know what it was, just that the one time he'd thrown up, he'd felt better all day. So from that day on, he'd not been drinking the nasty liquid.

"Is he dead yet?" This was a new voice, and Reuben told her it was Ward. A person she'd not meet either. "I hope to fuck soon. I'm getting sick to death of carrying around something that will kill me too if I accidently drink it."

"Then use the container that I gave you." There was a snort sound, and Reuben looked in that direction. Skylar could see him now. The name Ward now had a face as well. Dolin spoke to Ward as Reuben lay there with his eyes about half closed. "Margo will be dead soon. A matter of minutes, not days. This one...I fucking thought he'd be dead weeks ago. I told you we should have killed him first. Then Hector would be at our beck and call. We fucking need him."

"Not so much anymore. I think I've figured it out. With the help of Benton. Did you know that he's been experimenting while we were closed up? Anyway, he thinks he might have a way for us to duplicate the formula that will convert them." The voices faded, and she assumed that young Rueben fell asleep. But before she took her hands away from his head, there was another voice.

"I already told you two not to be in here while he's awake." The voice was low but had waked Rueben apparently. "What will he do if he comes back and the two of you are in here fucking with his son? Kill me too. How do I get you the information of his comings and goings if I'm not here?"

Rueben looked in the direction of the voice and there stood Mary. Before Skylar could pull her hand away and confront the woman, Rueben put his hand over hers. It was a different time when she spoke again, her dress was different as well. And from the position of the woman's in Reuben's vison, Skylar thought she had no idea he was awake.

"The woman is dead, but I'm thinking we need a new plan." There was a mumbled voice but nothing she could understand. "I don't care how dangerous it is. We have to find this kid's father and kill him too. Do you have any idea what will happen if the council finds out what we've been doing?"

"Not to worry, love. Once we take over the new world, we'll be sitting in a grand position." The voice belonged to Ward. "And once we have it all set up the way we want it, we'll rid ourselves of the dead weight and be sitting like king and queen on our own thrones in the new world."

"I'll take the kid to the house. I'm thinking I can get through their security. My sister, Ann, she works with them and there's no way she'll let me get turned away. I can feed you what you need to know." There was a long pause and a soft giggle. "I'll have to move soon. The wife is dead, and I don't know when Hector will get back. You can cover me with Dolin?"

"Yes. I have him eating out of my hands. And now that we can get the world cleaned of the people there, you and I will be rich beyond our wildest dreams." Another long pause and it occurred to Skylar that they were kissing. "Take the boy, but keep feeding him the blood in the milk. In a few days when he's gone for good, we can get the rest of the household there killed off and make our way past their forces."

When she pulled her hand away this time, Rueben let her. When he swayed slightly, she picked him up in her arms and handed him not to Mary, who was standing there with her hands out, but to Hector. He looked confused but held his son. Skylar looked at Mary.

"How long were you to wait before you killed the household?" She took a step back from her and bumped into Davis. He put his hands on her shoulders and held her there. "I've seen some really horrible bitches in my time, but to kill a woman and her child really takes the cake."

"I don't know what you're talking about." Mary looked at Hector, then at her sister. "Tell them, Ann. Tell them how I have cared for this child and his mother."

"I wouldn't lie for you back when we were children, Mary, and I certainly won't now. What have you done?" Mary looked at Hector when she could see that her sister wasn't going to be of any help.

"Master Hector, you have seen me with the child. How could you let her say these things about me?" She tried to pull from Davis's hands. "Let me go. This is just nonsense. I've done nothing wrong but care for your wife and child. Tell them that."

"How did she get the poison if not with your help?" The accusation from Hector was softly spoken but powerfully said. "My son too? How did someone come in and poison him if you were there all the time?"

The anger was taking over where there had been hurt and confusion. She was a good actor. Skylar would give her that. But when she took a step toward the woman to touch her mind as well, she screamed at them to let her go.

"I did nothing, I tell you. Nothing that any other person wouldn'd do for the man that she loved." Mary jerked from Davis's grip, and Skylar had a feeling that he let her go rather than she being strong enough to break his grip. "My darling is coming here and there is nothing you can do about it. Soon you will be fodder just like the rest of the humans here. We'll wallow in your blood and riches you left behind."

"Not for you." Remy put his hand on her shoulder, and the woman screamed. It was piercing in its intensity, and Hector turned with his son cradled in his arms. In seconds it was over. Mary was dead.

Chapter 15

Ward was sitting in his office when Dolin came in. He never knocked, and just as he was standing up to rip his ass open for not doing so, he could see by his face that something had happened. When Dolin sat down on the chair and simply stared at him, Ward knew as surely as he was sitting there that he was going to hate whatever he had to say.

"She's dead." Ward stopped moving toward him and stood very still. "Her body was returned here just a few minutes ago. With this."

Ward didn't want to touch the letter. He knew that as soon as he did, that as soon as his fingers brushed against the envelope, that the contents of it were going to be devastating. Sitting down in the other chair, he ignored the letter in favor of giving himself a few moments and finding out what Dolin was talking about.

"Who was returned to you? Was it Margo? I know for a fact that she's dead." Dolin shook his head. "Then who is it?"

"Mary." Ward was already shaking his head as Dolin continued. "One of the adherents brought her back. They didn't say anything but sat near her body while he sobbed. Then he gave me this before he pulled a knife and plunged it into his heart."

The envelope was still between them. When Dolin gave it a small shake, Ward reached for it but still didn't touch it. His Mary was gone. His sweet, sweet Mary was dead.

"Did he say who killed her?" There was no response and he looked at Dolin. The man was sobbing and it broke his heart just a little. Mary was the best thing that had happened to either of them. "Dolin, we'll figure out who did this and take care of them."

"Read the fucking letter." He took it then, as Dolin had shoved it into his chest. "That man did it. Rembrandt took her heart out and they didn't even send it back with her. Who does stuff like that?"

He wanted to point out that they did and had but only looked down at the sealed letter. "You didn't open it?"

"No. It's addressed to you. And I've been so grief-stricken that I just…just read it, Ward. Please? I want to go and bury what's left of our true love." Dolin walked to the window and stared out as he continued. "She loved you, I know that, but I have been in love with her since we were children. Her heart belonged to you, but she had mine as well."

Ward knew this. And it hurt him at times to know that Mary had loved him more than his best friend. But Ward also knew that she'd never have been happy with Dolin. They were a true couple since they had met all those decades ago. But because she was afraid of her parents, she and Ward had never married and now it was too late for them. He tore open the letter that was indeed addressed to him. The first line he read aloud.

"Hello fucking idiot." Ward looked up at Dolin when he laughed. "You wrote this? This is not funny. I suppose Mary is all right as well."

"No. I didn't write it and her body is now at my home. I have no idea why she was sent to me, but the letter with her was addressed to you. Go on. What else do they have to say?" Dolin sat down and stared at him. "I swear to you, I had nothing to do with this."

"All right then. But I swear to you if this is a joke, I'm going to kill you." He skipped over the greeting and read the body of the letter. "I'm assuming that by now we've figured out that you murdered poor Margo. Shame that, since she was the wife to my good friend, Hector. And so you know, Rueben is with us as well. You were fucking stupid for allowing him to see you feed him the poison. You should have drunk the dead man's blood yourself. Your death would have been much faster than what I've planned for you."

Ward got up to pace. If the kid was alive, then Mary had failed them as well. Her duty was to kill the boy there so that when Hector was in his grief, she was to kill him. This was so far not going according to any plans. Not even the backup ones they had thought of. He picked up reading where he'd left off.

"You should also be aware that we have evolved. Into what? We're still working on that. But according to Hector, and I trust him much more than I would you, we're stronger than any person or persons you have on your realm, as well as Benton. The next time I see him, he is going to be coming to your doorstep in a small baggie." Dolin laughed again, but this time Ward ignored him to continue reading. "The malefactors are dying as well. Daily we take out more and more of them. And if selling our agates to the highest bidder is all you got, then you are so fucked. Because of right now, they no longer work for your kind."

"Do you think that's possible?" Ward looked at Dolin when he spoke. He had to repeat himself before he knew what he'd said, as Ward was still trying to figure out how Rembrandt had found out about the stones. Mary would never have said anything, he was sure of that. "Ward, do you think it's possible that he's figured out that we need the agates?"

"I would think so." He looked at the rest of the letter before continuing. "It looks like he and Hector are best of friends despite the fact that he changed him to whatever he is now. What do you suppose he means about being evolved?"

"If he's stronger than Benton, we might have to do something else." *Really*, Ward thought. *And just what would that be?* "I've not heard from him since the day he took over the lab. Do you suppose they killed him?"

"I don't think so." In fact, Ward was positive of that. He'd heard from Benton just the other day and the man was not happy. And he was hurt. "You think that Hector really is working with them? He wasn't much of a team player with us. I wonder what changed his mind."

"You killed his wife." Ward nearly smiled. Okay, that was a good reason to turn on them, but it had been a necessity. A necessity that he was seeing now was not working for them. Other than the fact that he was no longer up their ass about every little thing, Hector was now spilling their secrets to the one person that could harm them. Maybe even kill them.

"We're going to have to go to the lab tomorrow. We have to work on something to ensure that Rembrandt and that bitch of his are no longer a threat to us." Ward wondered if Hector had contacted the other realms to let them know what had transpired but knew the man had no balls when it came to doing things that would require him to stand up to someone. "We're going to have to talk to our buyers as well. They will need to know that we have to hire someone to speak to them when they have questions. And tell them for the next...I would say a month, we'll be grieving for our dear Mary."

His Mary. Whenever he thought of her death, he wanted to curl into a ball and sob for her. He really did love her that much. But by the same token, her death might have saved them. The time they were going to use for their "grief" would also give them time to plan.

"Can you come up with something we can tell them? It will have to show our sorrow and what we're going to be feeling." Dolin asked him how he should say she was killed. "Not killed. Say she died of the flu we have here. And tell them while we're working on a cure for that as well, we're not making any headway. That way none of them will be tempted to come here for her services."

Dolin left a few minutes later, and Ward looked at the last few lines of the letter. The man had balls, he'd give him that. Reading them out loud gave him a thrill, a kind of scary thrill knowing that the man thought he could beat him.

"And I will personally rip you to shreds when I see you. I will not bother with asking you if you did it. For I know. And thanks to seeing just what you did in the mind of a small child, I will make your death be as long and suffering as I can. You are going to beg for your death before I'm finished with you."

"Not likely," Ward said to the room. "Not fucking likely. I will be the one to bring you down. As I have heard before, I created you. I will destroy you as well."

Instead of waiting until the morning, Ward made his way to the lab. There was too much riding on this, on all of their money, to wait. As he began to look around, two things occurred to Ward. He had no idea where to begin and even if he did, what the hell did he need to make it work?

~~~

Skylar was covered in blood. Not her own but of the creatures they'd been out killing. And it was as if they'd made very little progress in it too. There were still a great many of them coming out all the time. She looked at Remy, who looked as nasty as she did.

"We're not doing so well." He only leaned back on the seat and said nothing. She was exhausted too, but she was also afraid. "Will we be able to make a dent in the amount of malefactors made every day?"

"I don't know." Not what she wanted to hear, but he had told her he'd never lie to her. "We are going to need more people. And more practice at what powers we have."

She knew that as well. Every time she moved, it seemed as if she had something else to marvel at. Like today. She had been standing there next to a group of malefactors and when she put her wrists together to shield herself from their weapons, she felt the ground beneath her tremble and it knocked the creatures back, affording her time to kill them all. But there were more and more coming all the time.

The little burg they'd entered today had looked like a bomb had gone off. Not only were there dead bodies in the streets, but there were a few that were hanging out of their cars where they'd been pulled from them. They had also discovered that they were no longer concerned with going for the dying but causing accidents to change them. And few were being changed.

"What do you suppose the percentage is to them killing and converting?" Skylar looked at Davis when he spoke. "I mean, there was a houseful of dead bodies and the count matched what we thought were there. Do you suppose that they're killing more than their converting or the other way around?"

"I would say they are killing more than not. And they aren't just taking adults either." Davis had nearly been hurt when a small boy, about seven, had come at him trying to bite him. Skylar wondered what would have happened to him had she not stepped in and killed the creature. Remy continued before anyone else spoke. "I saw a dog today as well. They are converting anything and everything, it would seem."

Skylar nodded. She'd seen them too. Feral dogs that seemed more confused than anything. She tried to close her mind to all the carnage she'd dealt with today. There was just so much of it.

"We're going to need a great deal more help than the dozen that Hector said were coming. I'm thinking that a thousand times that isn't going to be enough." Skylar wanted to agree with Remy, but she was afraid to admit that she thought they were going to fail at this. "I will speak to him when we get home."

But when they arrived home, everyone was in the clinic. Catherine was having her baby. And as much as she wanted to tell the girl that this was not a good time to bring a child into the world, she knew that it was more than likely the best thing to happen here too. A little hope was what they needed.

Five hours after they got home and showered, little Carsen Jarvis Thomas came into the world weighing in at nine pounds and thirteen ounces. Skylar looked in on the little boy while the others talked quietly with the happy couple. Ann came up to stand beside her.

"He will be safe here?" Skylar hoped so but nodded at Ann. "I have been thinking on this thing with the others. How will we know them when they arrive?"

"We have their names. I'm just worried that there won't be enough of us to get this accomplished." The hand patting her on the back had Skylar smiling at Ann. "I'm very happy you and your family are here. I think little Carsen will give everyone something to smile about."

"As do I." She picked up her grandchild and handed him to Skylar. She declined but Ann insisted. "He will be watched by us all. You might as well get his scent. I wish for you and Remy to be there should he need you."

"We will be." But she took the child anyway. He felt good in her arms. Not nearly as light as she thought nine pounds would feel. Her hand touched his bare back, and he opened his eyes to stare at her. "He's wolf. And he's hungry."

"He more than likely is. But what else do you feel?" Skylar knew she'd been had. Ann wanted her to know the baby inside and out. "Tell me what I cannot feel from him."

Spreading her hand along his back, she let some of whatever her powers were spread over the child. He never made a sound but continued to stare at her. She felt as if he were reading her instead of the other way around. Then she touched on his mind, or his thoughts. The kid was talking to her.

"He wants to know if he'll be safe. He…Catherine told him of his grandfather and how afraid of him she is. Now he has a fear of him as well. Not for him but for his mother." Ann nodded, tears in her eyes. "He said that…he said to keep the doors locked and do not let him in when he comes. He is sure that he'll be coming too."

"I believe this as well. Do you feel that he has power to read people? As his mother and I have?" Skylar nodded and the little guy yawned. His voice, strong and so adult, told her that she needed to go to her resting place that things were going to get worse in the morning.

As Skylar handed the baby to Ann, she thought he looked sad. She wondered about that and nearly took him back to ask him, but he yawned again. Skylar yawned as well.

"We should head to bed now." Remy wrapped his arms around her as they watched Ann put the little boy to bed. "He'll be safe here. We'll make sure of it."

"I know he will. What I worry about is his future. What if we can't conquer this? What if…what if they keep coming and coming and we have no way to stop it?"

"We will." That really wasn't much of an answer, and she told him that. "I know, but speaking to Hector was fruitless. He said that help was on the way. And that once they were all here, we could see a turn in things. I told him if there was no turn soon, we'd all be dead. He assured me that we'd be fine."

For whatever reason, she didn't think it was going to be that easy. As soon as they left everyone to go to their room, Skylar stopped by the kitchen. It was empty, save

Hector. He was sitting in the chair staring out the window. It wasn't until she said his name twice that he turned to her.

"I was thinking of my wife. Margo didn't deserve to die like she had." Skylar sat with him as Remy got a glass and a bottle of liquor from the cabinet. As soon as the glass half full of the amber alcohol was sat in front of him, Hector looked at them both.

"Leonard is on his way. Once he gets here…he is not a person I would say will be friendly. He is sour to friends. I know not what has happened to him, but he will be hard to like at first. I would ask that you take a care in not harming him too soon." Remy laughed and she smiled. "I would ask that you not hurt him at all. I believe he is hurt enough."

"Physically or mentally?" Hector stood up instead of answering her. When he was out of the room, taking the glass to the sink and dumping it, Skylar looked at Remy. "What do you think?"

"I think he will fit in or not. Should he prove to be too much of a problem, I will feed him to the malefactors myself." He stood up. "Now. I should like to take you to bed and make love to you until we can no longer move. Then I should very much like to take you again, just to make sure that you are very relaxed."

Nodding, she stood up to follow him. But instead of her walking, he picked her up in his arms and carried her up the stairs to their room. Skylar let him hold her. She was simply too afraid to voice how terrified she really was. Her only wish was that she and Remy could stay together no matter what happened.

About the Author

Kathi Barton, author of the bestselling series Force of Nature, lives in Nashport, Ohio with her husband Paul. In addition to writing full time Kathi likes to spend time with her eight grandkids, three children and three children-in-laws. She writes to relax and have fun.

Her muse, a cross between Jimmy Stewart and Hugh Jackman brings them to life for her readers in a way that has them coming back time and again for more. Her favorite genre is paranormal romance with a great deal of spice. You can visit Kathi on line and drop her an email if you'd like. She loves hearing from her fans. aaronskiss@gmail.com.

Follow Kathi on her blog:
http://kathisbartonauthor.blogspot.com/

www.ingramcontent.com/pod-product-compliance
Lightning Source LLC
Chambersburg PA
CBHW032124170626
46808CB00006B/2091